Mo's Heart

A Miracle Interrupted novel

Edie Ramer

Blue Walrus Books

ISBN-10: 1939328063
ISBN-13: 978-1-939328-06-9

1

Mo had stepped into the kitchen for olives, and instead he was getting a show—most of it in his imagination. His favorite sous-chef headed toward him, taking off her apron while he took off her clothes with his eyes. Playing the same game he'd tortured himself with since the first day she'd marched into his recently purchased bar to welcome him to the small village of Miracle. A game he never won.

He'd done this so often he knew just how Rosa would look. Tall and regal, with wide shoulders and lush breasts. Then her slightly rounded stomach, her flaring hips and her long, sleek legs.

She frowned at him, as if she could see inside his mind and didn't approve. Her strong face matched her body and the spirit that her autocratic soon-to-be ex-husband hadn't been able to crush. Probably the reason he'd turned to younger, weaker women.

"Are you okay?" she asked, her husky voice sending heat through him.

"I'm always okay."

Her eyebrows rose and she touched his arm. The non-sexual touch—one she'd give a younger brother—sent more heat through him.

"You look tired," she said. "You've been working too hard. You need a break from the restaurant. You're here all the time. Don't you have any family you can visit?"

"Not nearby." He held his hand up to stop her from saying anything more. In the eyes of the villagers, he was a man to be admired. After all, he'd renovated the rundown bar with greasy food into a decent restaurant—with a karaoke stage—making it a gathering place for the villagers. He for sure didn't want her damn pity. "Don't worry about me. I'm doing fine."

She narrowed her eyes, shrugged her perfect shoulders, started to turn—and then snapped back. Stepped up to him. Hugged him. Holding him tight.

His brain froze, but his body fired up like the restaurant's pizza oven. For seconds, he felt her curves against his. Felt the first part of his fantasies come to life.

She released him and stepped back, her eyes...mysterious. "See you tomorrow," she said. Then she left, her hips swaying from side to side as if she were hearing a slow tango in her head.

He closed his eyes. "Tomorrow," he whispered, and it sounded like a prayer. "Tomorrow."

Then he headed to the pantry to get the olives. Because life went on.

Except for the occasional rumble of a semi driving down the two-lane highway that served as the village's Main Street, it was quiet outside when Mo sat at his kitchen table and prepared to type a letter on his laptop, just as he did every week. He sipped sage tea and thought of the way Dario looked the last time he'd seen him. Dario had only been fourteen then, young enough not to hide his anguish. Young enough to let Mo see that his heart was breaking. His eyes moist...

Until Theresa had taken him away....

Mo stopped the memories that had shimmered in his mind. There was nothing shimmery about it. Just blunt facts. If he'd stayed, he would be dead by now. Either ashes or his dead, bloated body on the bottom of the

Pacific Ocean, a hole in his forehead.

None of it mattered. He didn't believe in self-pity. When he'd let the FBI plant bugs in the two booths he saved for Leo and his men—The Di Luca Family—he'd known what the outcome might be. He'd done it anyway.

People made choices, and if he had to do it again, he'd probably do the same thing. At least he'd found a way to get letters to Dario in the last years. From a friend, to a relative, to another friend... Six transfers in all, but he'd been assured Dario got them.

In the last three years, he'd learned to be grateful for small things.

He bent forward, his fingers in place, and stared at the blank screen. He needed to shut up his mind, open his heart, and start typing.

Dario,

I hope you're well. Your mom, too. I think about you a lot. Even when I'm not thinking about you, you're in the back of my mind.

I can't tell you how much I wish you were with me. This village I live in now is tiny, but I've become a real part of it. The people here accept me. And though it's so different from Jersey, I accept them, too.

I can't tell you much about this place, not even where it is or what part of the country—not even the weather. I know you'd try to find me. You're hotheaded, the way I used to be. Now I'm the coolest guy in the place. So take your dad's word, finding me wouldn't end well.

If your mom is reading this, she'll see she'd be wasting her time to look for me, too. Besides, the way I set everything up, you two should be okay as far as

3

money goes.

What I can tell you about this village is that it's nothing like you see on a Hallmark TV show. Everyone isn't sweet and syrupy. Gossip is the number one sport. If there were MVP awards for gossip, we got a contender here. I'm thinking she could take home the top award.

I bet she'd give up half her bank account to know about me. It would make her year.

And just like in Jersey, people get drunk. Drive too fast. Fight about stupid things that no one gives a ziti about. Sleep with the wrong people. Get pregnant at the wrong times.

I hope you're listening to me. Seventeen is the age when you think you know everything. And you always were a smart kid. A lot smarter than me, that's for sure. You got those brains from your mom's side. I know she's told you to be careful who you poke, but you never liked listening to her.

Aw, Dario, I know you're thinking I betrayed you. That I cared more about Carl than you. But that isn't the truth. You're my son. And you're my sun. Without you here every day, I'm living in twilight.

Mo stopped typing to think about the one thing—one *person*—who lit up his days here in Miracle. It couldn't be, it would never be, but a man couldn't stop thinking. Or feeling. Even when he shouldn't. Even when nothing could ever come out of it.

Rosa Fabrini looked like a goddess. She even cooked like a goddess. And he...he was a man living with invisible ties that he'd vowed to honor. A man who could never give her his name. A man who wasn't even living under his real name.

His lips flattened together, and his mind shut out the useless regrets.

But you don't want to hear me whining like an out-of-tune violin. There are good people here, too. It's pretty much like every small town or village—except last fall something happened that pulled the villagers together. It was better than a Hallmark moment. It's something that doesn't happen much in Jersey.

He stopped again. This wouldn't be a bad place to raise a kid.... It was different here than in Jersey. Men in Jersey carried guns to kill people if it was necessary—and sometimes when it wasn't. Hell, he'd had a gun at the restaurant for protection; he thanked God he'd never had to use it. But here people carried rifles and shotguns to kill animals during hunting season. They'd sneer at someone carrying a paltry gun.

He looked back at the screen. These letters were always hard to write. He wrote them with half of his heart. The other half he'd left with a boy with brown hair and eyes, just like him, over a thousand miles away.

I can't say more about what happened. It's on the Internet and if I give you details I know you'll look it up and find out where I live now.

I guess I got nothing else to say, but if you could see into my heart you would know it still beats for you. Every night I pray for you and your mother. You are my world. I miss you like crazy.

Love always,
Dad

2

"I'm jumping into the pool," Rosa Fabrini said in the kitchen at Mo's Place, leaning against the stainless steel table. Pleased to take a mini-break, though she loved what she did. Loved the smell of garlic, tomato sauce, olive oil. Loved the slicing, the mixing, the baking. Loved the look on people's faces after they'd taken the first bite, their eyes half-lidded, their faces softer and brighter, as if they'd just had a taste of heaven.

"What pool?" Katie Guthrie, soon-to-be Katie Robbins, set a half dozen boxed pies on the stainless steel tabletop. It was Wednesday, soon the lunch hour would start, and Katie's pies went fast. Rumor had it there was magic in her pies. Not everyone believed, but one thing Rosa knew they all agreed on was her pies tasted like magic.

"It's snowing out," Mo said, carrying a container of frozen sweet sausages out of the industrial-sized refrigerator. "No one's swimming in this village for months."

"Not a swimming pool," Rosa said. "The dating pool."

Mo jerked to a stop and stared at her, his dark-brown eyes burning.

Rosa turned to Katie so he couldn't see her smile. He was six years younger than her, and it felt good to be desired.

Of course, if he asked her out, she would say no. She liked Mo, but the last time she'd dated a restaurant owner, she'd ended up marrying him. A mistake she didn't plan on repeating.

"Dating." Katie's nose wrinkled. "I'm so glad I'm through with that. You sure you want to jump in? There's some murky waters in that pool."

"I'll take care that no one gets any murk on me."

"You don't know what those guys are like out there." Mo set down the sausages. His tone was stiff, unlike him. "It's different out there now than when you were dating."

"I know how long it's been," she snapped.

"Hey, I didn't mean—"

"And I am aware of what the dating world is like," she said, cutting him off. She wasn't going to deny her years. She was proud of every single one. "I have two sons in their twenties and one eighteen. I listen to them and know."

"Not to mention her rat-bastard husband," Katie said.

"Ex-husband," Rosa said. "Any day now."

Katie shrugged. "He told Amber that according to the church he's still married to you."

"Is he trying to weasel out of marrying her? Very convenient time for him to remember our marriage." Rosa sucked in her breath. No sense getting upset about it. It would be over soon. "I really don't care what he told Amber. We went through mediation and agreed on everything. I signed the papers last week, and so did he. He's not my problem anymore."

"You're the lucky one," Mo said. "You found out the truth about him. That's something a lot of people don't find out until it's too late."

She looked at him, startled. His neck was corded, his jaw visibly clenched, his eyes looking at her and not seeing her, as if he were recalling an unpleasant memory.

"Who's your first dip in the pool?" Katie asked.

"Huh?" Rosa turned her attention back to Katie. "Oh, my accountant."

Katie's forehead wrinkled.

"He did my taxes this morning." Rosa put her hands on her hips. There was nothing wrong with an accountant. "He does the taxes for Fabrini's. He didn't know Mike and I split up until today."

"And he asked you out after doing your taxes?" Katie asked.

"He must've thought your figures were in good shape," Mo said, his tone rough.

She glanced over to see him glowering at the sausages. Laughter filled her, though she told herself not to be vain. But oh, how good it felt to know that she had an effect on this man.

"I think he thought my figure was shaped just fine."

Katie laughed, her hand over her mouth. Mo was turned sideways from Rosa, his head down, and his cheekbones flushed with color.

"When is your date?" Katie asked.

"Tomorrow night after work. I told him I won't get a day off until Sunday." Feeling Mo's gaze on her, she stood taller. "He didn't want to wait. He works nights during tax season, so the late hours are perfect for him."

"Where are you going?"

Rosa shrugged. "Out to eat. He said he normally doesn't eat well during tax season."

"Doesn't sound like a fun night," Mo said.

"It's so pleasant to work for an optimist."

"Work? Is that what you're doing?"

She turned her back on him. She knew the real reason why he was scowling, and it wasn't because she was talking to a friend. "If you're out with the right person, even a ride to the grocery store is a wonderful evening."

Katie's eyelids lowered, her lips soft. "If any of your pool dips are successful and you want to invite someone special to my wedding, I can make room for one more guest."

"Rosa works Saturday nights," Mo said.

Rosa shot him a look that should have felled him onto the concrete floor that was coated for easy cleaning. Right now, she would like to clean him right into the dumpster in the back.

"You may as well shut the place down on her wedding night. Half the village will be there." She turned back to Katie. "Make room for a guest. I'll bring someone."

A snort came from behind her, but Rosa didn't acknowledge it. She was tired of men thinking she couldn't do something. She could do anything she aspired to do.

At least she'd waited four months before jumping into the dating pool. She'd tried to realize an old dream of getting her own TV cooking show instead. She'd soon recognized that it had been a pleasant dream but she didn't care for the reality. She was still glad she'd tried it. Because of her, Katie met her videographer fiancé, and because of the other videos Gabe filmed, so much good had happened in the village.

"All right with me," Katie said. "One guest more."

She left soon before lunch hour opened. Scotty, the line cook, came in, and he and Rosa got busy for a long burst of time while they listened to bluesy songs on the speaker from Mo's playlist. He must've been in a mood when he'd made today's playlist. It had a couple of Marvin Gaye's slow, sexy songs like "Let's Get It On" and Barry White singing just about anything in his deep, bone-melting voice. And of course, Mo's favorite, Andrea Bocelli, whose voice was soulful and bone-melting in a different way. All the soul songs giving her multiple soul orgasms.

Finally the orders slowed, and she wiped the back of her hand over her forehead. Outside it was in the single digits, but it was hot in the kitchen.

Mo was heading toward the front with a handful of trash bags. "You sure you want to go toe dipping?" Mo asked, slowing.

She looked at him. He wasn't a beautiful man, but he had beautiful eyes. He was perhaps an inch or more taller than her. And he was thin and wiry where no one would call her thin or wiry, so it was good that she never aspired to either.

They were like coarse wool and silk.

Or chili pepper and chocolate.

The thought struck that if made by the perfect chocolatier, the chili pepper/chocolate combination might be deliciously combustible.

Heaven in her mouth.

She swallowed, aware that Mo was staring at her. Waiting for her answer. And she was looking at him in a way that she shouldn't look at an employer without asking for trouble. Not taking her eyes from his face, she cupped the left side of his jaw then pulled back, her fingertips trailing beneath his jawbone. "I plan on dipping much more than just my toes."

He gulped, his Adam's apple twitching, and she smiled serenely, as if her heart wasn't pounding wildly and her blood wasn't racing through her veins.

She turned her back to him and chopped onions, her head suffused with a fog that made his footsteps on the coated concrete floor sound like dull clods.

"Just be careful you don't go in over your head," he said.

Her head jerked up, and she glanced back at him. He stood with a hand on the swinging door that led to the bar, half turned to stare at her. From this distance, his dark brown eyes looked black.

Like he'd been to hell and back.

She knew what that was like. Since she'd found out about Mike and his infidelities four months ago, she'd spent too much time in that fiery place. Until the day she realized it wasn't the heat that was so horrible. It was the hopelessness. The destruction of her old life.

Now she was climbing out of that hellish place of anger and woe and self-pity, step by step, as she built her new life.

"Don't worry about me," she said, "I know how to swim."

The muscles of his face tightened, and he headed into the kitchen. She looked down and chopped faster, determined to enjoy her date, if only to prove him wrong.

3

"How did the dip go?" Mo stopped by the stainless steel table where Rosa stood, holding his list of things to do that he checked off one by one.

She glanced at him and he lowered his gaze to the list, as if her answer didn't really matter. And it didn't. Not really. He could never act on his feelings for her, and he wanted her to be happy. He just wasn't generous enough to want her to be happy with another man.

Through his eyelashes, he caught the instant she returned her attention to the dough spread out on the table. He dropped his show of indifference and openly watched her. The small shrug she made said everything. No words needed.

His tense shoulders relaxed.

"We ended up in his office in Tomahawk, and he ordered Chinese takeout. He had two clients to take care of."

"He's a jerk," he said.

She shrugged again, not in a normal American it-doesn't-matter shrug, but an Italian one that told him a dozen different emotions. The only one Mo cared about was that the guy was not someone she was interested in. Not someone who was a danger to Mo's happiness.

"If it were me," he said, "I would've told the clients to either reschedule or find someone else. That I had a date with the most beautiful woman in Wisconsin."

She turned to stare at him, her mouth dropped open. "Really?"

"It's the truth."

She frowned.

The muscles of his belly tightened. "Too bad I make it a policy not to date employees. I'd take you for a very long and very hot dip."

Her lips curved up, and she laughed, her eyes bright. She reached out to put her hand on his face, a gesture she did often, and it reminded him of his mom and his aunts, though they usually gave his cheek a pinch. Not Rosa. Once again, her fingertips caressed his cheek and his jaw before pulling back, leaving him wanting more.

"I'm in the employee pool," she said, her voice light with the same amusement that shone in her eyes, "so if we dated, that would be double dipping."

He groaned, and she laughed again.

"Too bad your evening was a bust." He stepped back, his skin still prickling where her fingers had lingered.

"It wasn't a complete bust."

"Oh?" He forced his shoulders to stay loose.

"While he was with the first client, I chatted with the second. An electrician." She smiled slyly, waiting for his reaction.

His skin, warm a few seconds ago, turned cold, but he raised his eyebrows, as if with mild curiosity, knowing what she was going to say before she said it.

"He and I are going out next Sunday."

"I hope this one works out better." He nodded and turned away. He'd had a small reprieve but had known it wouldn't last. There had to be a smart, single man out there who would find her and date her and treasure her.

He would be that guy...if he were single.

But he wasn't. She deserved her prince. When it happened, he would try like hell to be happy for her.

4

"How'd it go?" Mo asked in the kitchen the Tuesday after her date. She had the feeling he'd been waiting for her, like a cat waiting in the bushes for the squirrel to run down the tree trunk onto the grass. That he'd hovered in the kitchen, waiting for her to take off her coat before he pounced.

"It was...fine." She stopped in front of the refrigerator. Two dates and already she was sick of dating. "Fine."

"A bust, huh?"

She shrugged. "He's allergic to garlic."

"No one is allergic to garlic."

"He said he is. He said I smelled like garlic."

"Loser. You don't smell like garlic."

She wanted to ask what she smelled like to him. The thought warmed her skin. As if she would smell differently to anyone but him. "You say that because you probably smell like garlic, too."

"Nothing makes my mouth water more than the scent of good garlic. The guy is another jerk."

"He sneezed. Like I was dust or cat hair. I had him take me home early. We didn't even kiss."

"You wouldn't want to kiss him. He was no Prince Charming."

She laughed. Mo was good for her ego. If only he wasn't her employer...

But he was, and that was that.

"Are you planning on taking another dip soon?"

The bell rang before she could reply. He waved his

hand and set off to open the delivery door. She headed the opposite way, to the freezer. When she came out with ground beef, she stopped to avoid running into a dolly loaded with beer pushed by a tall man wearing a blue jacket and pants.

"Hey, Phil," she said. "How're you doing?"

"Hey, Rosa. I'm good. Business is good. Ice fishing is good." His half smile dipped. "The kids are good."

She remembered his wife had died from an aneurism a year or so ago, leaving him to raise two kids in their early teens. She'd sent flowers to the funeral home from her and Mike. She had to stop herself from making a sad face.

"How about you?" he asked.

While she chatted mostly about her sons, she sneaked a glance at his left hand. No wedding ring yet, but he was probably dating someone. He was about six four, and she'd been checking out his muscular arms for a year. The beer deliverymen did a lot of heavy lifting, and Phil's body showed it. His hairline was receding, but his smile was nice. She'd take a nice smile over good hair any day.

"Your divorce final yet?" he asked.

"Pretty soon." She didn't want to go into all of Mike's petty maneuvers to get her to give him more than his share. It wasn't going to work. He was the one who was expecting a baby. He was the one with a timeline. And just days ago, he'd finally given in.

The thought made her feel lighter. Made her want to laugh and dance and flirt. Though the divorce wasn't finalized yet, she was single in her mind.

"You miss being the boss lady?"

"No way. I'm enjoying being just the sous-chef." As she said it, she realized how true it was. No more twelve-hours work days for a small wage—because she'd thought

Fabrini's was her place as well as Mike's, and the profits would be for both of them.

How stupid she'd been. How trusting.

She would never trust like that again. Of all the many reasons she had to hate Mike, that was the big one. He hadn't broken her heart; he'd stolen her trust.

"So, are you seeing anyone?" He smiled casually, but tension gathered around his eyes.

That feeling of being desired and desirable slid up her spine like warm olive oil. Her lungs seemed to swell, her breaths easier, and she shifted to jut her hip as she smiled at him.

"Not at the moment."

"Would you like to do something with me?"

"I work Saturdays."

"So do I. I'm off Sundays," he said.

The back of her neck heated. Without looking behind her, she knew Mo was watching her. Staring at them. Straining to hear her answer. Hardly able to breathe.

Or was that what she wanted to think?

"How do you feel about garlic?"

"The more the better."

"Good answer. I'm off Sundays, too."

"This Sunday? We could go out to eat and a show."

"I'd like that."

He took her phone number and had a big grin as he pushed the dolly past her and to the cooler.

She grinned, too, heading toward the prep table. When she'd decided she was ready to date, she'd wondered if her age might make it harder. Apparently not.

Maybe Phil would be the one. After all, he did like garlic.

5

Rosa was quieter than usual on Tuesday, with an air of sadness that cheered Mo and at the same time made him feel lousy.

She didn't talk about her date on Sunday, and he didn't want to bring it up again. He couldn't stand it if she guessed how he felt, and if he kept asking, she would know. Talking about dates was something women did with other women, and guys with other guys. They were the same sex and understood each other. Maybe gay guys were different, he thought, as he poured draft beers for the four Branski brothers. Gay guys could talk to women and men. When he'd been single, his gay cousin had been his go-to guy for advice on women.

He wished he could call Rick and ask his advice right now. But, no, he'd avoided calling anyone with a Jersey area code for almost three years now. In the beginning, it felt like he'd cut off his arm, but he'd resisted the urge. Besides, he knew what Rick would say. Rick was always one for taking chances.

Once upon a time, he'd taken chances, too. Not this time. This time there was too much at stake.

The night got busy, the speakers playing La Boheme until the open karaoke started. Opera wasn't the usual bar/restaurant music, but this was his place, and if anyone had the bad taste not to like it, they could eat someplace else. By nearly seven, there was a lull in the food orders, and Brenda took his spot behind the bar so he could grab something to eat in the back.

It just happened to be the same time Rosa clocked

out. Before she left, she usually chatted with him for a few minutes.

When he got to the back, he grabbed a plate of Rosa's lasagna. In the break room, Lisa, the other waitress, was counting her tips. If he'd known she was here, he wouldn't have left the front. There were too many diners for Brenda to take care of it alone.

"You going back soon?" he asked.

"In a minute."

He sat down. A minute wouldn't hurt.

He heard footsteps on the floor outside. He could tell by the way the soles struck the floor in a confident half strut that it was Rosa. Inside the break room, her gaze went straight to him. Her lips curved up before she turned to Lisa and the loose pile of bills and coins.

"A good night?"

"Let's just say I'm a happy girl tonight." Lisa put the bills in the pocket of her black apron. "What about you? How was your date on Sunday?"

"I'm beginning to think dating isn't for me." Rosa turned her back on them and stepped to the closet.

"That bad? Did he try anything funny?"

"There was nothing funny about our date." Rosa put on her black coat as she talked, turning back to face them. "His daughter called and said she was sick. We drove to his place, and he accused her of faking it to keep him home. I said she looked sick to me, and maybe I should call a taxi. He said she pretended to be sick all the time, that she was just like her mother."

Mo's hand tightened on his fork. "Her mother?"

"You didn't know? Phil's wife died of an aneurism a year ago."

"And he said that?" Mo asked.

"Jesus." Lisa slid the coins into the pocket with the

bills. "You meet all the winners. And then what happened?"

"His daughter threw up on him."

Lisa laughed. "That must have stunk."

"Everything about it stunk. I took a taxi home. At least he paid for it."

"Did he ask you out again?"

"I didn't give him much encouragement. I told him he deserved it."

Lisa laughed again. "I'm surprised he paid for your taxi."

"I think he was embarrassed. I felt sorry for him— until he said that about his wife."

"I almost feel sorry for the guy." Lisa stood.

"I don't." Mo's neck heated with anger. "A good man doesn't say things like that about his children's mother. I've got a mind to ask for someone else to deliver the beer."

"Don't." Rosa's forehead creased with concern. "It would just make it worse. I had the feeling he doesn't date much and was nervous. I felt bad for him."

"After you said he deserved it?" Lisa asked.

She laughed without any humor in her voice. "Well, he did. But he doesn't deserve getting in trouble at work."

The heat in Mo's neck cooled. "He's lucky you have a tender heart."

She pushed hair back from her face and grimaced. "Not that tender. Just ask Mike."

"I wouldn't believe anything Mike said about you. If he said your eyes were brown, I'd double check before I agreed with him."

She looked at him but didn't say anything, and Mo felt the tension stretch between them, like a string tightening on either end of their hearts, and from the speakers came Charles Aznavour singing one of the greatest love songs of the world.

And then the song stopped. Mo blinked and sucked in his breath, filling his belly, the invisible string that was only in his mind broken.

Except Rosa was blinking, too, shaking her head, as if she also felt it.

He glanced at Lisa, who looked from Rosa to him, her eyes narrowed and her mind adding up more than tips.

"I'd better go." Rosa hurried to the door, pulling on her gloves. "See you tomorrow."

"Take care," he said, and turned back to his lasagna.

Another song came on, this one from the karaoke. He recognized the singer: one of the Herscher girls, cute in a pixyish way. Her boyfriend was probably staring at her the way he'd just stared at Rosa.

Lisa stood in an abrupt movement that sent her blond ponytail swinging to the side. "Why don't you ask her out?"

He looked up at this bright-eyed young waitress who wore too much makeup and was saving her money to go to cosmetology school. "I think you're past your break time. You've left Brenda alone too long."

With a laugh, she snapped around to the door that led to the bar, her ponytail bouncing. "Men. They're so stupid."

He turned his attention back to the lasagna, not arguing with her. He was stupider than Lisa knew. Stupid enough that someone wanted to kill him.

6

The phone trilled, jerking Rosa out of a deep sleep on Saturday morning, her eyelids snapping up. Grayish sunlight seeped into her bedroom from the edges of the blinds. Too early for anyone to call her unless something was wrong. Wide awake, she lunged for the phone on the nightstand, the fear that the call might be about one of her sons putting all her senses on alert.

She'd never been a worrier until she became a mother. With her oldest twenty-five and the youngest eighteen, she doubted she would ever stop worrying.

Sitting up, her bare arms chilly, she said hello.

"Guess what?" The voice of Linda Wegner, town gossip extraordinaire, made Rosa clutch a fistful of the purple spread she'd bought after Mike left with the brown one she'd never liked.

"Just tell me."

"It's good news."

Rosa still clasped the spread. Linda Wegner considered the worst news the best news. The more to talk about. The more dirt to spread. Rosa suspected that talking about Mike's infidelity had given Linda more orgasms in the last four months than any her husband, Dean, had ever given her. In fact, the news had probably given Linda more orgasms than any Rosa had gotten from Mike.

Amber wasn't the only woman Mike had gotten pregnant young. At least Amber was in her twenties and had a lot more experience than Rosa at nineteen.

"I was sleeping," she said.

"You won't mind me waking you when you hear my news."

Rosa shifted the bedspread higher and drew her knees up. "What?"

"It's about Amber."

"I really don't want to hear about—"

"Her baby isn't Mike's."

Rosa's mouth dropped open, and no words came out. Questions tumbled in her mind, but she slammed them back.

"Don't you want to hear more?" Linda asked.

"Do I? I'm not sure if I care."

"Of course you care." Linda's tone was shocked. "This changes *everything*. Don't you at least want to hear who the father is?"

"Sure." Rosa made her voice disinterested. It made no difference to her if the baby was another man's...but it would make a difference to her sons. And Linda was the only one with enough nerve to talk in detail.

Of course, Linda wasn't calling out of good intentions. She called solely to get Rosa's reaction.

Too bad for her that Rosa didn't feel particularly generous this morning.

"It's the Tomahawk boy she was dating. The one who moved to Green Bay to work with his uncle last year."

"Hmmm."

"Turned out he came back for a weekend to visit his family. They got together, and you know what happened next."

"Hmmm."

"Aren't you more interested?"

"I can guess. He found out she was pregnant—maybe a mutual friend mentioned it. He called her, and she told him the baby really was his. "

"No! Nothing like that."

"Oh? You sure?"

"Of course I'm sure," Linda said, her voice sharp enough to cut paper.

Any other time, Rosa would've smiled. But right now she thought of the poor sucker from Green Bay and felt a little sick.

"He wasn't sure if he believed her. He'd found out she was sleeping with Mike when they were together. But then his parents heard it might be his, and they're the ones who paid for the paternity test."

"So, the baby is his. Now they're getting married?"

"He doesn't want to marry her. He's engaged to someone else, and they want to adopt the baby."

"You're joking." Rosa shook her head, and now she did smile.

"I know! Isn't it delicious?"

"It's...interesting."

"She's back at home with her parents, who aren't too happy with her. Mike kicked her out of their place late last night."

Rosa glanced at her clock on her bedstand. Six oh five a.m. "How did you find this out?"

"A birdie told me." Linda made chirping sounds.

"You know a lot of birdies."

"Well, I am at Wegner's all day. The Anything Store. Anything you want, we have."

Rosa nodded. Especially gossip. Linda's husband took care of the stock and the accounts. Linda took care of the gossip.

"You should apply for a job with the CIA. You're the best."

Linda's laugh tittered out, pitched high with giddiness. "If I were younger, I'd try out for the E cable channel. I'd share all the latest celebrity news."

"I'm sure you'd be great."

"Thank you. Not enough people appreciate what I do."

"I think enough people do. If not for you, more people would go to Wal-Mart in Rhinelander instead of shopping locally."

"That's what I tell Dean. The people around here will go anywhere that's cheap. It's the German in us. Dean has it, too."

"I'm sure. Well, I have to get up now. I suppose I appreciate you calling."

"I knew no one else would, and I thought you of all people deserved to know."

"Yes, me of all people." Rosa heard the flatness in her voice.

"So, how do you feel about it?"

"Like I have to pee."

"No, how do you really feel? Mike will probably go back to you now."

"Not if I have anything to say about it." As soon as the words were out, Rosa made a face. After all her restraint, Linda had gotten what she wanted. Her one honest reaction that told Linda everything about her bitterness, her anger, her hurt feelings.

Not that she was hurt anymore, but the other kaleidoscope of emotions… Maybe a little bit.

And maybe a lot.

She hung up and hurried to the bathroom. It was going to be a busy day.

7

Wegner's seemed to be busier than usual so early in the morning, and twice Mo squeezed around a few women who huddled in the aisles, whispering, their carts lined in a row.

Someone must've done something stupid last night. Whatever it was, he'd hear about it at checkout. Linda Wegner looked happier than usual this morning, bending over the counter to talk to a gray-haired man who was buying cat litter and bending closer to hear whatever she was saying.

The gossip this morning must be like the hamburgers Scotty sometimes made after being inspired by one of his favorite cooking shows: extra juicy.

Mo put on his not-interested face, though he wasn't above keeping up with what was going on. After all, he'd chosen to be part of this nowhere village where no one could find him. And where no one wanted to kill him. And it wasn't as if gossip was confined to small villages. In the part of Jersey he'd come from, there'd been as much gossip as hair spray.

One of his waitresses at his Jersey restaurant had told him she'd read in a magazine that gossiping was healthy. It showed you cared. If that were true, Linda Wegner had to be one of the most caring people on the planet.

He had to stand in a line before he could check out his grapefruit and bananas and a bag of chocolate chip cookies. He liked his sweets, and the sweet potato pies that were supplied by Katie Guthrie, the local pie baker, had sold out last night. He made a mental note to order more next time.

After greeting five people by name and chatting with the woman behind him, he realized he knew everyone in the place by name. In Jersey, he didn't even know the name of everyone who came to his restaurant.

Sophie Butler, whose husband, George, owned the Butler Hardware and Bait Store—one of only two black families in the otherwise all-white but not squeaky-clean village—nodded with her long chin to let him know he was next. He thanked her and turned—only to find Linda Wegner narrowing her eyes at him, as if he were a piece of meat she wanted to cut up and throw on the grill.

Then she smiled, and it was a predator's smile.

She smelled gossip.

He steeled himself. What had happened that involved him?

A thought made the hair on the back of his neck stand straight up. Did the Di Lucas find him? Were they in the village right now, asking about him? Smiles on their sallow faces. Loaded guns in their pockets. Murder in their hearts.

Schooling his face to show no expression, he plopped the bananas and grapefruit on the counter, being more careful with the cookies.

"So." Linda smiled at him, not even making a pretense to do her job. She wasn't a bad-looking woman: a couple inches shorter than his five nine; a clear complexion; blue Germanic eyes and blond hair. A little stocky. But to Mo, it was the avidity in her face and eyes that made her unattractive.

Right now, her scandal-seeking radar was aimed at him. He braced himself.

"Did you hear about Rosa?"

His eyebrows rose. He'd been stiff before, but now he

stood so rigid they could put him in the gusting wind outside and stick a flag on his head.

"Something happen since last night?" he asked.

Linda cackled. "I'll say something happened. Then you don't know about Amber yet."

It took a second for him to recall that Amber was the skank who Rosa's husband had gotten pregnant. "Nothing."

"He's not the baby's daddy."

A shockwave rocked him, but he managed to stand without swaying. "Huh." He scratched his head and pretended it didn't matter. By the way her smile changed into a frown and her shoulders hunched forward, he could tell he'd succeeded.

"Everyone's saying he'll want Rosa back now."

He shrugged, unable to talk, his jaw locked. His fingers curling at his sides where she couldn't see.

"The restaurant's not doing as well since she left. Mike had to hire two people to take her place."

"Well, she's a great cook and a good worker."

Her frown deepened. She emanated frustration in hot waves. "He'll want her to quit your place."

"I guess I'd have to hire someone else."

"Doesn't that bother you?"

He finally got it that she knew how he felt about Rosa. Lisa had probably confided her suspicions to a friend, who confided it to others.

Soon Rosa would find out.

Shit.

"Yeah, it bothers me. She's a damn good sous-chef. Makes a killer lasagna. And her cannelloni..." He kissed his fingertips then raised his crabbed hand heavenward. "I don't know who could replace her. But if it's what she wants, I'll be happy for her."

Linda's face crumpled. As if he'd grabbed all her sparkling hopes for gossip fame in his fist, slammed them onto the floor, and then stomped on them until every twinkle winked out.

Scowling, she checked out his items and put them in a bag, giving him a look that sent him bad juju vibes.

Too late. He strode away from her. *I've got more bad vibes than you've got gossip.*

Outside Wegner's, he trudged to his place on the next block, the below-zero February gusts biting his ears. He headed straight to the side door and upstairs to the bigger of the two apartments above the bar. He passed the smaller one that he used to store Christmas decorations and strode to his place at the end of the hall. He'd turned down two offers to rent the smaller place; he just didn't want the hassle of being a landlord. Besides, he was with other people most of the day and the evening. He needed some alone time. Especially during times like this.

In his kitchen, he dumped his bag on the table and sank into a chair, his elbows on the tabletop, his face in his hands.

He wanted to yell. He wanted to swear. He wanted to pound the table with his fists.

But he prided himself on his control, and he sat like that for long moments until the fear loosened its grip on his throat and he could suck in a long breath of air. Only then did he lift his head and look at the ceiling.

"God, if you're there listening to me, I hope you'll do whatever is best for her. We both want that, don't we? I gotta say, though, that cheaters like her husband... Well, I've known quite a few, and they just don't change. You know that. I know that." He gestured. "You think I'm just saying this because I want her and can't have her. That isn't so...."

He paused a moment, thinking this out. He didn't talk to God often—usually just to curse or ask why. But this time he wasn't doing it for himself. This time was for Rosa. He wanted it to matter.

"It's true I like her a lot, but I'm not a safe man. Rosa deserves a man who can be here for her. Who's not ready to take off if the wrong guys come into town. And who will be faithful. Faithful is important. So keep it in mind, will you?"

Then he got up to put the groceries away before he went downstairs to prepare for the rush of diners for lunch and then more at night. The karaoke crowd came out in full force on Saturday night, so they would be packed.

He'd see Rosa later this morning. He wondered what he would say to her.

He wondered what she'd say to him.

Christ, he felt like a high school kid, and that was only a good thing when you were talking about your eyesight.

8

The sun was still climbing up the sky, and Nick was breaking Rosa's heart.

Nick was her youngest. Her baby. Sensitive. Not as tough as the older boys. He was the clingiest son, the neediest. The one who'd spent a lot of nights in his bedroom after his dad moved out. When she asked what he did there, he said, "Pray for Dad."

She wanted to ask, "What about me?"

She never did.

And now his prayers had come true.

"I think Dad's going to come back now."

Instead of answering right away, she stirred the kettle filled with the no-name-soup she and a thousand other Italian cooks made without a recipe. Just chicken broth, tomatoes, whatever beans and vegetables she had in the pantry, lots of chopped basil and Italian seasonings, and of course, garlic. Sometimes she threw in pasta. Sometimes something else. Wherever the whim took her.

Her kitchen smelled like Italian heaven.

But behind her, she felt her son's agitation. Nothing heavenly about it.

Her nervous energy had inspired her to make the soup for her and Nick to eat tomorrow on her day off. Now that energy was seeping away.

With a sigh, she set down the spoon and turned around.

"He can't come back. Our marriage is broken."

"It's not. Father Ted thinks the most godly thing we can do is to forgive one another."

"I forgive him, but I won't live with him."

"Mom, he made a mistake." Sitting on the stool by the island, Nick held out his hands, palm up, this boy-man who alternated between hating his dad and loving his dad. "Everyone makes mistakes."

"That's right, but it was his mistake and he has to live with it. Not me."

"Mom, he thought he was doing the right thing. He didn't know what Amber was like."

"He was married. That was the right thing? To have sex with her? And now he's blaming her?"

His cheeks flushed. "That's not what I meant. I meant when he thought she was pregnant."

"It's exactly what I meant. I was his wife, and he cheated on me."

"Mom, you're *still* his wife. He's *still* your husband."

She shook her head. How many times could her heart break? It felt as if every sentence coming from him was a knife thrust in her heart.

"And he's still my dad."

"Divorce won't change that."

"It changes *every*thing."

She put her hand up to her forehead. This was going to get ugly. "It wasn't the first time he cheated."

"He said you would say that."

Her hand dropped, and she went still, staring at her son. Tall and dark and handsome like all her babies, he was just a little slimmer, just a little more handsome. The girls called him all the time, and when he started dating at thirteen, she worried while Mike felt only pride that his son took after him.

"So you talked to him about this already?"

"He's my dad. This is his house. The house he worked for. I think he should move in."

"The house *he* worked for? You mean I didn't work for it?"

"Not as much as he did."

"Really." She crossed her arms and leaned back against the stove. "Tell me more."

"Why should he pay rent? You know the place isn't doing as well since you left. He can't afford it. And you should go back and work for him instead of that other job."

She felt the frown lines crease her forehead, and for once, she didn't quickly smooth them in fear that they would stick. "Do you really believe any of what you're saying? That I contributed nothing? That I didn't do as much as your dad?"

His gaze slid away from her face. "I just want you and dad to get back together. I want my life back."

"I wish you could have your old life back. But it's not happening. Is that what you told your father when this all began?"

"Mom, I keep telling you." He raised his eyes again, straight at her, his face so earnest it made her chest hurt. "Dad's sorry for what he did. He's trying to put it back together."

"It's too late. This isn't a broken vase. It's my life. And I'm not going to live the rest of it with a man who can't be faithful."

"Mom!"

She flung her hands up in the air. "Look, all this time I've avoided saying anything to you about your dad."

"I know what you thought." His lips curled slightly. Sullen.

"Nick, that's enough." She gave him The Stare that snapped him and his brothers into obedience. The one that her friend Katie called her Secret Weapon.

This time he glared harder. "See? You do that to Dad, too. Make him feel like he's never going to be as good as you. No wonder he wanted to be with Amber. She didn't make him feel inferior."

She stumbled back until her backside hit the stove. Her heart pounding and her eyes prickling, she leaned against it to keep from sinking to the floor as she stared at her handsome son. Seeing in his face the anger and mutiny.

"Does your dad make you feel inferior?"

"No!"

Heaviness was like a large stone in her chest. "Sweetie, as much as you want to turn our life back to what it was, it's just not going to happen. He cheated, and not just once."

"But, Mom, as soon as you found out, you were the one who told him to get out."

"You're right, I did. How do you think I felt? What if it were different? What if I was the one who cheated? Would you be asking your dad to forgive me? To take me back?"

He glared at her, this son who sprang from her loins. Glared at her with hate and heartbreak.

That made two of them whose hearts were broken. "You're dating men now."

"That's right. And I'm not defending myself." She put one hand on her hip. "Or would you rather I be like your dad and date women?"

"You're making fun of me!"

She sighed and put down her hand. "I forgive your father, but I don't respect him or love him anymore. Most of all, I don't want to live with him."

He jumped up. "Then I don't want to live with you."

She looked at him, and she could feel her heart

cracking into tiny pieces, raw grief burning through her. "In that case, perhaps you should start packing your clothes."

"I hate you," he said, the same thing as when he was seven and she wouldn't buy him his own TV so he wouldn't have to watch his brothers' shows. But his eyes weren't filled with tears now.

Hers were.

His flamed hate.

She walked toward her own room, her steps heavy. But a tiny bit of hope remained. With every step, she expected him to call her name. To tell her he was sorry. That he really didn't mean it.

But when she turned into the bedroom, he still didn't call her name.

9

Nick left with her favorite purple suitcase filled with clothes in his car. He didn't speak to her, and she didn't speak to him.

She didn't cry. The tears were locked inside her chest, and she knew when they did come, there would be a waterfall of tears. It would be like Niagara. But she felt frozen now. Frozen from the inside out.

The house felt empty, too big for her. She wished this had happened later in the morning. On Saturdays, she didn't start work until one p.m. instead of her usual eleven a.m. Rosa normally liked the later start and didn't mind staying later. After the separation, before she started working for Mo, Saturday nights were always the hardest. Nick worked at his dad's, and she was home alone. It was not the way she had envisioned her life.

None of this was how she'd envisioned her life.

She put her soup in the fridge, then she cleaned. As if she wanted to erase every footstep Mike had taken in the house. Every breath.

After a two-hour whirlwind of cleaning, every surface shone, and she had nothing to do but wash her hands and collapse in the purple easy chair that filled the space where Mike's recliner used to sit. The one item of furniture he'd taken with him.

She picked up a book. A romance. Probably not the best book to read now. She thought of calling her mother who'd gone back to Italy after Rosa's dad died, but in their last conversation, her mother told her not to divorce Mike. That their marriage was sacred.

If her marriage was still sacred after Mike slept with other women, then she should be able to sleep with whomever she wanted.

An image of Mo popped into her head. She imagined him naked. His wiry body so different from Mike's heavier body. Mo had a body like an athlete.

Her skin warmed and her heart thundered, and the blood in her veins felt like it was thickening and slowing. She even felt lightheaded, the way she did when a slow song came on at Mo's, and she would look at him and see the darkening of his eyes. As if his thoughts were liquid sex.

And she had to turn away and remind herself that she didn't do bosses anymore. That she wasn't going to repeat the mistake she'd made when she was young and impressionable.

He and Mike had nothing in common except their Italian ancestry, their dark hair—though Mike's was threading with gray—and their sallow skin coloring. And they both owned a restaurant. Proud dictators in their own little worlds.

Dictators didn't make good husbands.

But it wasn't a husband that she wanted now. Right now all she wanted was good, healthy sex. A man's body against hers. Something that would make her feel alive for a few minutes. Something that would make her forget for an hour—or ten minutes, if he was anything like Mike—that she was going through hell.

For a second, she worried she might not be Mo's type with her voluptuous curves and her height. She was as tall as him. And in certain places, she had more body fat than he did. Not that she thought she was fat, but what woman wanted to weigh more than her lover?

The horrible, horrible thought for some reason made

her crave chocolate, but she curled her fingers tightly and held herself back from going into the chocolate drawer.

And what about the six-year difference between her and Mo? It didn't seem important. She felt more passionate now than when she was young. Filled with juice.

The images in her mind made her skin heat. Of course she wouldn't do anything with him, but it didn't hurt to daydream.

A maroon car caught her attention, and she recognized her real estate agent's car slowing in front of her house. Easy to recognize since Gloria was the only real estate agent in the village.

Was she showing the house? Gloria should have called first, but luckily she had cleaned.

Her life was a mess, her house was spotless and shiny—and she'd prefer the other way around.

Gloria stalked out of the car in her calf-length wool coat and a stylish black knit hat that had Rosa stepping closer to the window to see what it looked like. No one else exited the car, so Gloria wasn't showing the house, which was too bad. Not many people in Miracle could afford this place with its high-end design pieces and the extra acreage, with the lake in back of them. Any buyers would have to be from out of the village. Mike certainly wouldn't accept an offer too much less than what they were asking.

Gloria bent over the For Sale sign, and Rosa frowned. If they'd had an offer, Gloria should have notified her.

With a quick movement, Gloria yanked up the For Sale sign. Rosa watched as she slogged toward her car, lugging the sign with her.

Rosa dropped the book and ran to the front door, her slippers slapping the wooden floor. She tugged open the door. Frigid air rushed in as she called Gloria's name.

Gloria turned, her mouth twisted, clearly not happy to see her.

"Gloria, what are you doing?" Rosa shouted.

"Ask Mike," Gloria called.

"What?"

"He came to my office and took it off the market."

"He can't do that. Not without my permission."

"Honey, I can't get in the middle of this, even if I do think he's a douchebag."

Rosa clenched her teeth and curled her hands into fists, no longer sad as hell. Just mad as hell. "I could kill him."

"If I had ten dollars for every time I heard that." Gloria shrugged. "Get out of the cold and call your lawyer. But don't tell the douchebag I advised you."

"My lawyer's on her honeymoon."

"Call her as soon as she gets back. Whatever possessed a divorce lawyer to marry? You'd think she'd know better."

"Maybe she's in love."

Gloria snorted.

"I know she wants children."

"You don't have to be married to have them. You don't even need a man. Just pay a sperm bank. Oh well, I suppose she has an airtight prenup." Gloria lifted the sign with both hands and waved it at her. "Good luck." she said before trudging to the car.

Rosa's teeth chattering, she closed the door. She stepped into the living room, grabbed the throw off the couch, and wrapped it around her shoulders.

She was going to kill the controlling, lying bastard.

So far she'd played nice, but she knew his recipes. She could...

She stopped in the middle of the living room, as if one more step would take her into an abyss of darkness. Nothing. She could do nothing to him. Not without hurting her kids.

The only way she could hurt him would be through his pride.

A way began to form in her mind. Like the tiniest wiggle of a worm about to be born... A man's image inside her head. In this case, born again.

Mo.

Her thoughts had been going back to him this morning already. Like a robin returning every spring. A hungry robin. A horny one.

In her mind she could see the yearning in his face as he looked at her sometimes when he thought she didn't notice.

She noticed. She always noticed.

If she had an affair with him...

Really, why not do it? So he was her boss. She was smart enough to keep it to an affair. He was hot for her, and she admitted she was hot for him. Why not jump into that fire? Fast and eager—and naked.

Only three reasons not to do this. Her sons. It was bad enough they knew about their father. They didn't need to know about her, too. And in this village, of course they would hear. After she found out about Mike, she'd discovered that everyone else had known for years. But no one had told her. Not even Linda Wegner.

Matt was in New York, and he wouldn't know. If he did, he'd understand.

That cut her reasons to two.

Tony, her middle son, was living in Tomahawk now. He was the earthiest of her sons, the most in touch with his primal self. She had the feeling he would understand.

So that cut her reasons to stay away from Mo to one.

But Nick... The only thing he understood right now was that his parents had screwed up, and he was in emotional pain.

She wrapped the throw tighter around her, and her breath shuddered out. What was she going to do?

10

Dario,

I hope you don't mind getting another letter from your dad so soon. There's a gossip storm going on in the village. Remember what the restaurant used to be like? I would joke that it was like a small village, and sometimes the villagers misbehaved. Multiply that by 500 and that's what this is like.

What kills me is that someone I know is suffering.

'Course, what really kills me is that I'm missing you so much.

I just want to be there for you. You're the sun and the stars to me. I hope you're listening to your mom.

I hope you're taking care of yourself.

I hope you'reeeeeeeeeeeeeeeeeeeeeeeeeeeeee...

Taking his hands off the keyboard, Mo closed his eyes tightly. As if squeezing out the sight of the office.

Usually he slogged through the days. He had to be philosophical. Things happened, and with his emotions, he had to be the Zen guy sitting on top of the mountain.

But it wasn't easy holding on to the Zen-like state when he was the guy in the middle of the action. The guy greeting people, making menus, handing out drinks and paychecks, making friends, having ideas. Even in Miracle. The reason he'd taken out the old pool tables and put in a karaoke machine and a small stage. Nothing earth-shattering, but the old bar hadn't done so badly. He could've left it. Served bar food and a lot of beer.

Made enough to get by.

That's all he expected in life now. Getting by.

Yet he hadn't settled. He'd worked under other chefs, other restaurant owners, the only job he knew. Living cheaply, saving his money, moving on every few months when the howl started inside him. Like a lone wolf torn from his wolf pack.

Then one day, driving down a Wisconsin highway, he'd seen a place that needed to be fixed...and he'd fixed it.

Back in Jersey, he'd tried to fix what had gone deadly wrong, and his world had fallen apart.

Some days were worse than others. This was one of those days, when he wanted someone so much it hurt.

Someone who felt right to him every time he saw her.

But she was married and might even be going back to that asshole.

And if that wasn't enough to keep him away, he was married, too.

What the hell was he going to do?

The sound of the back door closing woke Rosa from the light sleep she'd fallen into on the couch, a pillow under her head, a throw wrapped around her.

Nick! He was back!

Joy wiped out a lingering sadness, and she half rolled, half fell off the couch, the throw tangled around her legs. The footsteps stopped in her kitchen. And by the time she freed her legs and tossed the throw on the couch, a sense of dread took the place of the joy.

The steps were too heavy to belong to Nick.

She walked slowly forward.

The man in her kitchen wasn't her slender, tall,

handsome son. Instead it was her stockier, medium-height, soon-to-be ex-husband.

"Mike, what are you doing here?" She raised her chin and strode boldly toward him, hearing the old adage in her mind, *Don't let them see you sweat*. Only she substituted *weak* for *sweat*.

She should have known this was going to happen. Known that Mike—the jerk, the douchebag, the asshole, the arrogant cheater and liar and manipulator—would walk into her home as if nothing had happened. "Our agreement specified that I live in the house until the divorce is finalized."

"Baby, there is no divorce." He smiled at her, and though he still retained some of his good looks, to her he was the ugliest man in Miracle. Which was saying a lot, because there were some doozies in the village.

But the others weren't ugly on the inside. Not like the man standing in front of her with a confident smile on his face that made her want to kick him. Hard. In his special place.

"This is a legal agreement," she said. "I'll contact my lawyer."

"She's on her honeymoon."

Rosa sucked in a deep breath. Her lawyer's marriage to a major furniture store owner in the area had been on the news. Even their plans to spend Valentine's Day in Paris and then travel to Italy and Spain.

"Besides, what happened was a big mistake."

"Your big mistake." She crossed her arms and gave him The Stare. "And when you make a mistake, you have to pay for it. The bigger the mistake, the bigger the payback."

"I did pay for it." He held out his hands and still kept his smarmy smile, but she could see the coldness in his eyes that looked like tiny, dried-up walnuts. "I didn't have you."

"You still don't. Get out."

"No." He shook his head, pressing his lips together into a thin line. "I've been thinking, and it's best for everyone that we get back together. This hasn't been good for the kids."

"You mean Tony and Matt lost all respect for you."

He glared at her, not pretending anymore. "They sided with their mama."

"Don't blame me for that." She shook her head at his denseness, though what she really wanted to do was shake him like he was a filthy mop. "Isn't it ever your fault? Do you think you can walk through mud and it won't stick to you?"

Now his lips curved down, and he had a close resemblance to a bulldog about to bite someone. "Mud washes off."

"Think again. Whenever I see you, I see mud."

"In that case, you'll be seeing a lot of mud. I was wrong to do what I did, but now I'm sorry. I admit it. I want you back. In my house—"

"*My* house."

"My bed," he continued, as if she hadn't said anything, "and my restaurant."

"You're insane."

"Not insane. I'm doing what's right for this family. We split up this family—"

"*We?*"

"You didn't fight for me."

She shook her head. This man had no conscience. He would do what he wanted and blame any problems on her.

"You can't say you were the perfect wife."

"You mean I wasn't twenty years younger."

"Age had nothing to do with it. It was your attitude. I talked to Father Ted, and he's relieved that the divorce is off."

"Stop! Stop, stop, stop!" She put her hands over her ears then took them off. "I want you out of here. Leave right now." She pointed at the back door.

He didn't budge. "If you would only use your common sense, you would know I'm doing what's right for you."

"I'm not listening to you anymore." She stepped past him, toward the counter and heard him follow her. She grabbed her cell phone and turned around to face him. "The only thing that's right for me is you leaving. If you don't walk out of here right now, I'm calling Jerry."

He held out his hand. "Don't bring the village constable into our business."

"Are you nuts? Your business is all over town. If you don't think every man and woman in Miracle is laughing at you now, you're mistaken."

His eyes blazed, and his hand whipped up.

She stilled, not taking her eyes off him, the same way she'd look at a rattler in her living room. "You hit me, and I'll have you taken to jail."

He lowered his hand. "I wasn't going to hit you."

Her heart pounded wildly. "You just raised your hand to wave goodbye? That's fine with me. Walk out now. Before you embarrass yourself more."

His eyes burned into hers, then he did just that. Left.

She didn't release her breath until the door closed again. Her breaths shallow, she stood in the living room, watching out the large window as his sedan roared down the street.

Her body started to shake. Her breaths came out in gasps. She slumped onto the couch, wrapped her arms around herself, then rocked back and forth. Finally she got up and headed to the kitchen to call the nearest locksmith and have all the locks changed.

If that didn't work and he still tried to come back, then she would have to leave. Her pride hated the idea and rebelled against it. But the pragmatism that came from her mother and her mother's mother before her, and probably ran down from generations of women in her family who bore children and married imperfect men, trumped her pride.

In two and a half weeks, her lawyer would be back from her honeymoon and would sort this out.

She was stubborn, she was heartsick, but she swore that she was *not* going to live with Mike ever again.

And after that, she needed to get to work. She had a couple hours before going to work to start prepping. If she was late, she'd have to move like a crazy woman. Which would be fine. It would match her crazy life.

11

Mo poured glasses of wine to the book club ladies sitting at the long table in the back, all ten of them. Though they didn't sell out during Saturday lunches, they usually had enough diners to make Brenda hustle for her tips. Today was just about right.

Scotty was whipping out the sandwiches and soup in good time. Mo headed to the kitchen to see if he needed help. Since Rosa wasn't in, he grabbed a knife and started slicing tomatoes and onions. A recovering alcoholic, Scotty told Mo when he came in an hour ago that he was moving in with his new girlfriend who was a recovering meth addict. Mo had congratulated Scotty and hoped it worked out. The girlfriend had her own Internet business and was moving to Miracle. Cooks came and went, sometimes faster than the seasons, and Mo didn't want to train a new one.

"She cooks Italian food," Scotty said, a tall, overweight guy who smelled like nicotine. "Maybe she can take over for Rosa."

Mo cut his finger, the pain quick and deep. He swore.

"That don't look good. Better put a bandage on it." Scotty wrapped a towel around it to stop the bleeding.

Gripping the towel ends, Mo remained in front of the table. Not even the stinging pain stopped him from finding out what Scotty meant. "What makes you think she's not coming?"

"Haven't you heard? She's going back to her husband."

It took a moment for Mo to answer. He felt as if

someone had slugged him in his stomach. "Who told you?"

Scotty shrugged his shoulders, and his belly shrugged, too. "Everyone."

"Does everyone have a name?"

Scotty frowned and then laughed, a hahaha laugh. "I get it. You're telling me that 'everyone' isn't a name. Let's see..." His eyes rolled up then down.

Mo waited, his nerves tightening by the second. Though Scotty was a good line cook, he wasn't the most brilliant guy in the world. But Mo suspected the most brilliant guy in the world might make a lousy line cook.

"I stopped off for cigarettes at Wegner's, and that's where I heard it."

Mo breathed easier. "Can't always trust what Linda says."

"Nah, it's not Linda. Mike Fabrini came in and said he was moving back in. It was before I was there, but everyone told me about it. You look pissed."

"I'm not pissed." He was hurting. But he was not pissed.

Not yet.

"Then I guess it's true," Mo added. With a nod, he went back to the office for a bandage. His hand shook as he put the bandage on his finger. He felt as if the world was spinning out of control. He should go back up front. Brenda might have some drinks he needed to pour.

But instead, he picked up the phone to call Rosa. Only he didn't call out. He held the phone in his hand against his chest for so long that the "if you'd like to make a call" message started twice. And he just sat there like that for moments, the phone beeping at him.

He wasn't going to call her. He should go back to the front. More diners might have come in. He needed to put down the phone and head out front.

But then he pressed number two on his speed dial. Number one was the fire department, which he hoped he'd never have to use.

Number two was the only one with a name.

On the fourth ring, he was about to hang up when Rosa answered. "Mo," she said. "Do you need me early today?"

Was that a hopeful note in her voice? "Not unless you want to work for free."

Her laugh was husky. He closed his eyes and imagined she was in front of him laughing, her luscious mouth parted, her eyes lit up, her face glowing with pleasure. And he could smell her, a combination of olive oil, garlic, and the sexiest woman he'd known.

"I don't work for free." There was a pause while he still smiled slightly and thought of what to say about the reason he'd called her. "Not anymore," she said, her voice different. Flat.

"I've been hearing things—"

"Oh?" Now her tone was acidic.

He'd been right. Not a good time to call her.

"Forget it."

"I will not forget it. Tell me why you called."

Her anger cheered him, and his tensed muscles relaxed. This was not the voice of a woman reconciled with her husband. This was the voice of a woman who wanted to butcher him then put him through a meat grinder.

"I just heard you were going back to work for your ex." As he said that last, he frowned. They weren't exes yet. Not officially.

"Listen," she enunciated clearly, as if making sure he heard, "I am not going to work for Mike. I am not going to stop the divorce proceedings. I am not going to live with him."

"Good."

"Yes. Very good. I'll be there at my usual time."

"If you need me for anything, call me."

"I won't need you. I am *not* a needy women."

She hung up before he could tell her that everyone was needy at one time or another. But it didn't matter. Not now.

It was okay. She wasn't going back to Mike. She was still going to work with him, though it didn't change anything else. It wouldn't stop her from taking more dips in the dating pool. A woman as beautiful and wonderful as her would find a different man to love her. He hoped a good man next time.

And he...he would go on the way he had before she worked for him. Just getting through the days. With nothing to look forward to except glimpses of Rosa.

But not yet, thank God. Not yet.

12

Rosa wanted to kill Mike. This time she was awake when Mike returned. And this time he didn't leave his Buick in the driveway, this time he parked it in the garage. She watched from the living room window and cursed herself that she hadn't changed the code on the opener. And she cursed herself for not having new keys made after he moved out.

But how could she think that he'd do something like this?

She thought all of this as she called Jerry, the village constable, and told him to get there quickly.

She waited for Mike in front of the door that opened up to the garage. In her hands, she held a broomstick. He had called her a witch. She'd damn well show him what a real witch did with a broomstick.

She knew where she wanted to stick it.

The door opened, and Nick stepped into the large hallway.

"Nick?" she asked. "You came back with your father?"

"It's his house."

"The divorce agreement stipulates that I live in the house."

"But you don't need to be divorced anymore." His mutinous expression told her he knew just how furious she was. How close she came to using the broom on his head. When she'd never hit him or his brothers. Never. Instead she'd just grabbed them and smothered them until they'd wiggled away from her, laughing so hard that snot came out of their noses.

She missed that little laughing boy.

"It's that woman's fault," Nick added.

"Really? Is it that woman's fault when your dad, a much older, married man cheated on me?"

"Yes."

"You know what? I don't like you very much right now."

"Rosa!" Mike's voice boomed. "Is that the way you talk to our children now that I've been gone?"

He was in her house. With two suitcases.

She pointed the broom at him. "I called Jerry. Leave now. You're embarrassing yourself more than you've already embarrassed yourself."

His complexion reddened. "You look like a witch."

"Good. I know how you hate witches. I want to be everything you hate. That way we can hate each other equally. Go back to your restaurant and find another twenty-year-old waitress to fuck."

"Mom!"

She gave Nick a look that should have shrunken him a few inches. "You never heard that word before?"

"Not from my mother."

"Okay, I take it back." She turned to Mike. "Go back to your restaurant and find another twenty-year-old to take to your bed and show off your inadequacies." She shifted to smile tightly at Nick. "Is that better?"

"No, it's not better!"

She frowned. "No? Tell me, how would you phrase it?"

"Amber was twenty-eight!"

"Those eight extra years make it okay to cheat on his wife?" She jabbed a finger at him. "And don't you dare say she made him do it. Unless you want me to tell you about all the other women who tempted him. Since we split up, I've heard of five more. There was—"

"Rosa! I order you, don't say another word to my son."

"Why, you—" She raised the broom over her head as Nick shouted at her to stop, and Mike's face turned the color of a turnip. Hers heated with anger, too.

That's when the door to the garage opened again, and a tall, spare man about thirty stepped in. "Hey, folks. Having a family reunion?"

Rosa lowered the broom.

"Jerry," Mike said, "good to see you, but there's no need for you to come."

"Yes, there is." Rosa gripped the broomstick tightly to stop her from lunging at Mike and putting her hands around his neck. "Jerry, thank you for responding so quickly to my emergency call. Mike and I are getting a divorce. We've already been through mediation—for which I had to pay half—and we signed the papers. Now he's trying to renege to salve his pride. I'm sure you heard what happened between him and Amber."

He grinned, his brown eyes that matched his buzzed hair laughing. "Sure did. Heard about it from at least six people. It's the talk of the village." He slapped Mike's shoulder, reminding Rosa how much she always liked him. "Too bad, Mike. Guess it happens to the best of men."

"And the worst of men," Rosa said with a smile that caused Nick to frown and Mike to narrow his eyes at her in the way he used to do when they were married. Letting her know that she was going to hear about her actions later.

Not this time, she thought. Not ever again.

"In the mediation, we agreed that I get the house and he gets the restaurant. And I was being generous there, just because I wanted it over with." She glared at Mike. "They're legal documents, and he has to leave."

Mike smiled, a smarmy smile that the president of the bank in old movies used before forcing the heroine and her family into the street. "You don't have all of your facts straight. Remember, I had to leave early for the restaurant and was going to sign it later?" His smile never dipped. "Well, sweetheart, later never came."

"I don't believe you." Her fingers felt numb, and so did her brain. As if someone had shot it up with Novocain.

"Ask your lawyer. She called last week to remind me to sign it and send it right away." He shrugged, still smirking. "I never got around to it."

Rosa closed her eyes. Feeling lightheaded. Knowing from his self-satisfied expression that he wasn't lying.

"Rosa?" Jerry asked. "Do you have a copy of the agreement with his signature?"

Her eyes still closed, she shook her head, her heart thudding, feeling the hard pulse of the vein in her neck.

"Then I can't do anything to help you. You'll have to talk to your lawyer. Sorry."

Not as sorry as she was. She opened her eyes, refusing to look at Mike or Nick. Just Jerry, his mouth screwed up and his eyes pitying her.

"Jerry, will you wait for me while I pack my clothes?"

"Mom!"

"Rosa, don't be stupid."

Jerry nodded. "Sure, I'll wait." He turned to Mike and Nick. "I would appreciate it if you two would stand back."

"She's my mother!"

"She's my wife."

"That doesn't mean either of you own her or can tell her what to do. So back up, boys." The steel in Jerry's voice surprised Rosa in the midst of her pain as he continued. "Unless you want me to charge you with harassment."

"I think you're making that up," Mike said.

"Why don't you call your lawyer and ask him if I'm making that up?"

Still standing in the office, with Jerry's body a buffer between her and two of the four people who were supposed to love her most, she heard heavy breathing then the tick of the grandfather clock from the living room. Then Mike stomped by her to the kitchen. To call his lawyer, she presumed. To see if there was another way that he could legally screw her.

"Nick," Jerry said, his voice low and gritty, "think about what you're doing. Your mother needs people who support her right now. You're going to look back at this in a few years and feel like crap about yourself."

"Why don't you mind your own business? Don't tell me what to do. I'm not a kid anymore." He stomped off after his father.

Rosa closed her eyes. Another stab in her heart. Nick was getting better and better with his aim.

Jerry turned around, sympathy in his eyes, and she dredged up a smile. "I won't be long," she said.

"I'll go with you. Make sure no one tries to stop you."

She appreciated his presence behind her as they strode past her glaring son and Mike on the phone, glowering at her with the full force of his disapproval. She raised her chin. In the hall, she stopped by the big closet to pull out the suitcase shoved in the back. Jerry pulled out a second one for her.

While she packed in the bedroom, Jerry stood in the doorway, guarding her. "Make sure you take everything you need," he said. "I'd bet money that the first thing

Mike will do after you leave is change the locks. Don't rush because of me. I'll make sure you'll be okay and no one will hurt you."

She nodded, not bothering to say that it was too late for that.

"Do you have somewhere to go?" Jerry asked.

She glanced up and smiled, though it felt like she was baring her teeth. "A place Mike won't like at all."

Jerry laughed as she finished packing. She'd thought her life wasn't going to get worse, but maybe, after all, it might get better.

Because when you hit bottom, there was no place to go but up.

13

Scotty's curious glances toward the back hall told Mo something was off. He turned and saw Rosa. She looked wan and tired and was still the most beautiful woman he knew. At her feet were two suitcases.

He grabbed a towel to wipe his hands. They were near the end of the lunch rush, but after their slow start, more diners than usual had come in. A snowstorm was supposed to be heading their way tomorrow, and people were doing their shopping and their dining out before they were buried in the white stuff. Brenda and Lisa could handle the front and pour their own drinks, so he'd hopped behind the grill to help Scotty out.

"You'll be okay?" he asked Scotty.

Nodding, Scotty scooted over to handle the whole grill.

Mo headed over to Rosa and looked straight into her eyes. "What's wrong?"

"You can tell?"

"I'm psychic." He tapped his head.

Her lips tipped up into a smile, though her usual light in her eyes was deadened. "I thought the word was psycho."

"That too." He wanted to hug her, just to comfort her. But not with two waitresses liable to walk into the kitchen any second and the dishwasher and Scotty around. The gossip would be all over the village by the time lunch hour was over, even if he meant the hug as a gesture of comfort.

"The suitcases were a good clue." He gestured at

them.

"Mike moved into my house, so I moved out."

"That's not right. He should be the one to leave. Call Jerry."

"I did. Apparently Mike never got around to signing the agreement we'd mediated. I don't know why my lawyer wasn't on him for that. She's known for her shark reputation."

"My favorite kind of lawyer."

"She promised me marriage wouldn't make her into a sheep." She rubbed her forehead. "Maybe it was the wedding preparations. Never mind. It's done, and I have to move on. It will work out. Other women have it worse."

He fought another urge to hug her. She looked so forlorn and yet was so brave.

"Right now it's not other women going through this. It's you, and you have a right to be pissed."

"I'm more than pissed. I'm furious." She gave a laugh that held no humor. "What use would it be to rant and rage? I did all of that when I found out about Amber. Carrying that bitterness was like a ball of poison inside my belly. It hurt me more than it hurt them. And my kids..."

She trailed off. Except for the sounds of the kitchen and Scotty calling out to Tim, the busboy, there was silence while she scrunched her face, as if she would cry.

Mo held his breath. If tears did roll down her face, he would have to hug her. And if he hugged her...

"I won't do that to myself again," she said, her voice low and fierce. "Being independent and happy... *That* will be my revenge."

"Good for you." He nodded his approval.

"Not good, just practical." She gestured in the air, a

change-of-subject twist of her hand. "Anyway, my lawyer is gone for another two and a half weeks. I wondered if I could stay in your extra apartment until she gets back and takes care of it."

He stared at her, his heartbeat speeding in a happy dance while his mind jabbered at him, saying it was a bad idea. A very bad idea.

She held out her hand, half turning away from him before he could say anything that made sense. "Never mind. I'll go to a motel in Tomahawk. I should've done that right away. I just thought—"

"Yes." He curved his fingers over the shoulder of her black coat, the wool thick under his palm and fingers. "Yes, you can stay in the apartment. I have the Christmas decorations stacked in the living area. I'll have to move them."

She turned back and laughed, but there was a wobble in her laughter. "You just took them down two weeks ago."

He shrugged. "Nothing wrong with Christmas in January."

"Leave them where they are. My lawyer will be back soon and sort this out."

"You're dealing with the legal system. Plan on at least twice that length." He grimaced, remembering something. "The apartment is probably dusty. I think it was clean when I moved in. I've never cleaned it since."

"In that case, it's definitely dusty. Don't worry, I know how to dust."

"And the refrigerator." He grabbed her two suitcases, ignoring her sound of protest, pulling up the handle of the one with wheels, lifting the other one without wheels. "It's probably older than I am."

"Like me," she said with a choking laugh that sounded

close to a cry.

Her woebegone expression tore words out of him. "Not anything like you," he said, hearing the gruffness in his low voice. "I never once had to fight my urge to kiss a refrigerator."

Then he headed past her, hearing her gasp before it was drowned out by the rumble of the suitcase wheels. Then came the thumps of her footsteps as she rushed to catch up to him.

He led her into the break room then down the short hall to the side of the house. No one locked their doors in Miracle. No one but Mo. He had too much Jersey in him...and too much to hide. He never knew when someone might come into town, see him and recognize him. Unlikely, but according to the residents, unlikely things happened in Miracle. So he set the suitcases down and got out the key.

All this took less than a minute but it seemed like much longer with Rosa so close behind him. She smelled like exotic spices. He wondered if he sucked on her skin what it would taste like.

Heaven, he thought as he climbed the stairs that led to the two apartments above the restaurant. And it was going to be hard as hell to stay away from that taste of heaven.

14

The apartment was cheerless, but Rosa pushed back her instant dismay. The previous owner was an old bachelor whose whole life was hunting, fishing, and talking with other hunters and fishermen. Decorating wasn't his thing, or else he had a penchant for brown and dreary.

At least it was clean, and all she needed to do was dust and vacuum, which she'd do anyway. Gloria had made Fred pay for a thorough cleaning before she would list it. That story had given the villagers a few guffaws.

She turned to look at Mo bringing in the suitcases. How odd to think that seven months ago, she hadn't known him. It felt as if he'd been in her life for...well, forever.

All this ran through her mind in a second as Mo stopped beside her. "It's not a palace."

"I wouldn't know what to do in a palace."

"You'd be the queen. Anything you wanted."

She laughed, surprised by his comment. Surprised that she had laughter in her. "I'd rather be a cook."

"You are that. The best sous-chef in the village."

There was a quiet moment between them, and a sense of peace sighed inside her as she looked at his serious face and knew he saw her as a strong woman, a woman who was temporarily down but not out. Never out. Not as long as she had breath.

She stood taller.

"The furniture is pretty ugly," he said.

"I don't know. The couch is the same color as your

eyes."

"Do me a favor?"

She looked at him. He never asked her for favors. "Of course."

"Run downstairs and get my chef's knife and bring it back up here."

She laughed again and felt a shift inside her. Like she imagined the earth felt when a boulder in a precarious spot moved. "Why?"

"So you can gouge my eyes out."

Her laughter spilled out as she shook her head. "Now that I look at your eyes," she squinted at his face, "I can see I was wrong. They're more like the color of...hamburger. Well done hamburger."

He grinned. "I was hoping for chocolate."

"Milk chocolate," she said immediately, then took a better look and saw their depths. "No, dark chocolate. Not just any kind. Truffles. With the beautiful, creamy center that you bite into and close your eyes and feel the bliss."

His left eyebrow lifted. "Are you flirting with me?"

"Me? Never."

The wry look he gave her, as if he saw through her act to her heartbreak, brought back the sadness with a heavy whoosh.

"We should change apartments," he said. "This isn't good enough for you to stay in."

"No," she said, but he was already turning with the suitcases.

What was it with men not listening to her?

Whatever was going on, she was ending it now.

With a quick move, she grabbed his wrist, his skin warm beneath hers. A current sparked between them, shocking her. He started, and she saw he felt it, too.

She dropped his arm. It must have been the carpet and the dry air.

"I'm staying here." She ignored the breathiness in her voice. "No arguments. I'm not a delicate flower. Or a queen. And I won't be an object of pity."

One side of his mouth curved up. "Pity isn't what I feel when I look at you."

She stared at him, her skin heating, her breaths shallow. Muted sounds drifted through the floor. Someone laughing, then others joining in.

But louder than the voices were the wild beating of her heart and the rush of blood surging through her veins.

His eyebrows rose, and she stepped back, as if he could read her emotions. But of course that couldn't happen. Without a word, he headed to the bedroom, carrying one suitcase, the wheeled one rolling crookedly behind him.

She stayed in the living area. She wasn't sure what was happening to her, but she was sure that following him into a bedroom wasn't a good idea. Not the way she felt now.

Oh God, what if this was the first sign of menopause? The sudden heat, the palpitations, the weak knees? She thought she was too young, but it wasn't something she'd researched.

And she'd heard that women in their forties got a burst of estrogen. Their bodies saying, *This is the last chance, lady. Get it while you can.*

He returned. "Take anything you need for cleaning or food or anything. I have extra sheets in a closet." He nodded his head toward his place. "The door's unlocked. I only lock the outside door and the one to the break room."

She sucked in air. "Do you have an extra key?"

"I think so. Somewhere." He tried one pocket then the other. The second time, he came out with a key. "You keep this for now. I'll look for the spare later. I've got to go back. I know no one locks their doors in Miracle—"

"They do when they have a restaurant downstairs and money from receipts," she said, taking the key, feeling stronger, more like herself. "We're trusting in Miracle but not stupid."

His cell trilled. He pulled it out of his pocket. Looked at it. Grimaced. Put it back in his pocket. "Gotta get back to work."

"Thanks for everything," she said, and watched him leave.

His footsteps thudded down the stairs. Then came the sound of the door to the break room opening and closing, and she still stared at the empty doorway.

And all she could think of was what she'd said about him looking at her. *Pity isn't what I feel when I look at you.*

Her skin warmed again, and she was pretty sure it wasn't menopause.

Oh Lord, she was in trouble.

And she liked it.

15

"How's Rosa doing?" Brenda asked, a mom of three in her thirties. She was Mo's most colorful waitress with a chubby body, short hair streaked with black and pink, and tattoos that today's long-sleeved black top covered.

"She's all right," he said.

"Told you," Scotty called out from the grill. "Rosa's a tough one."

Brenda rolled her eyes. "You men are so dense. She's not tough, she's proud."

"Proud is worse than tough," Scotty said. "Pride is a sin. A deadly one."

"I never got that. I think it's stupid."

"It's in the Bible."

"Your Bible."

"Hey! I believe in that Bible."

"I've seen the way you drink. You believe in Captain Morgan."

Tim, the busboy, laughed.

"Not anymore," Scotty said. "That was the old me."

Brenda shrugged. "I keep forgetting. Sorry."

"Is this a gathering?" Mo asked. "You having an employee meeting without me?"

"Hey, I'm working." Scotty grabbed an order, leaving only two more.

"It's a lull," Tim said.

Scotty slapped two more hamburgers on the grill then finished up another one. Mo watched him for a minute. The rhythm had changed in the short time he was gone.

There were only two more orders up. Soon it would be time for breaks and chatting then preparing for the Saturday night rush.

"It's going to be busy tonight," Scotty said, putting the burger up for Lisa to grab.

"Yeah, tomorrow's snowstorm." Mo took a step toward the front.

"Not the snow. Rosa."

Mo snapped around. "What about her?"

"Not her. It's the others." Scotty's orange eyebrows lifted. "Haven't you been here long enough to know that everyone will be coming to see if she looks happy or sad? They're hoping she'll step into the restaurant—you know, like she often does—and confide in someone. Even if the snow comes early, they'll be here."

"Maybe they'll go to Fabrini's."

"Too expensive." Scotty shook his head, as if pitying Mo for his massive ignorance. "Don't you know by now that the people around here hate shelling out money even more than they love gossip?"

Mo held up his thumb. "Got it now. Cheap and gossipy. They should make it a town motto."

Scotty laughed. "Nah, according to our illustrious village board president, our motto is to 'do nothing because no one likes change.'"

"Gloria's on the board, right? When I bought this place she told me the village motto was something to do with progress."

"You always believe what anyone tells you?" Scotty asked. "I'll remember that the next time I hit you up for a raise."

Mo raised his eyebrows. "I'll remember that, too."

The door to the restaurant swung open. A tall, thin man with long, white-streaked black hair strode in, wearing a leather jacket and holding a pie box. "Hey, Mo. I hear Rosa's staying in the empty apartment upstairs. Brenda said I could go in this way."

Mo shook his head. Something strange was happening to his plans to build a restaurant and not get too close to anyone. He'd thought he would be an observer. Instead his place had turned into the village hub, the woman he lusted after had moved into the apartment next to him, and the local weed grower was bringing pies to her.

"Hey, Sam." Scotty grinned. "You bringing gifts to Rosa? You're the first."

The first of wannabe suitors, Mo thought. Instant gloom slammed down on him, like a dark cloud in a cartoon. He nodded at Sam. "Sure, I'll walk you to the stairway."

"No need. I know the way. Thanks for taking her in." He nodded at Mo, and Mo wanted to ask who the hell Sam was to thank him for doing anything to Rosa. His daughter and Rosa had done a video show together, but as far as Mo knew, they had nothing else going and they weren't related.

He watched Sam head into the break room as he told himself it was none of his business. He wanted her to be happy, and if Sam or any other guy could do that for her, he'd be the first to wish him well.

Still, he needed to find the other key to the upstairs so he could lock the damn door.

A slap hit his back, and he jerked forward before turning to glare at Scotty.

"You gonna call Rosa to warn her?" Scotty's eyes were warm with sympathy.

Mo looked away. So he knew. Or guessed. He wondered how many others guessed.

"I should." He got out his phone, feeling suddenly nervous, like a teenager calling a girl.

Only he'd called plenty of girls before he married Theresa, and he couldn't remember any of them. Right now he felt as if his brain had been sautéed by one gorgeous sous-chef who could cook almost as well as she looked.

Rosa answered, and when he told her about Sam, she said she could hear him knocking. Her tone changed, and he guessed she was walking to the door. She said he was probably bringing one of Katie's pies.

Mo bought Katie's pies to serve at his place. They tasted a hell of a lot better than anything he made. In fact, they tasted a hell of a lot better than desserts at his old place, and that was a four-star restaurant while this was a joint that wouldn't get any stars from the big rating places.

"I hope it's a Change is Good Pie," she said. "Hey, Sam." Her voice rose then lowered. "I have to go."

Mo put his phone away and returned to the front of the place. His stomach was knotted, and he was glad to go back to work. Glad it would be busy tonight. Glad he was here to help Rosa.

He wanted more, but he'd weathered worse things, and he would weather this.

At least no one in the village was trying to kill him.

16

Rosa walked into the dining area at the end of her shift with her big-girl smile on. She still received looks of sympathy and pitying stares. She raised her chin. If anyone was brave enough to mention Mike's name to her, she would very sweetly bring up something that went wrong in their life. At one time or another, *everyone* had something wrong in their life. In Miracle, it was public knowledge. Because that was the thing about Miracle. If she did a cartwheel on her front porch in the morning, everyone would be whispering by dinnertime about the color of her panties.

Only now she had no front porch. And no one was going to have a look at her panties.

She stopped at the end of the bar where Mo was filling up a tray of drinks for Lisa. On Saturday nights, he was everywhere, moving fast. Being the host, the bartender, the restaurant owner. If he had to, he'd cook and wash dishes and wait tables. Rosa had seen him do it all. Never looking tired, as if driven by adrenaline and, from the way he ate her food, garlic.

He glanced at her, his eyes unreadable in the dim bar light, and she shivered, her skin warming. As if her body knew something she didn't.

The heat lingered when he looked away to set the last drink on Lisa's tray. Lisa took off and he turned to say something to one of the Belcher brothers sitting at the bar.

She stepped farther into the room. From the karaoke stage came the unmistakable off-key voice of one of the

Schilling girls destroying a Christine Aguilera song. Like most of the Schillings, the voice sounded like a rusty pipe trying to spit out water.

The feeling that she was being stared at brought Rosa's gaze back to the bar. The dozen people sitting on barstools were gawking at her as if she were a hurt puppy and they were waiting for her to whimper.

She lifted her chin again then stepped to the waitress stand and raised her hand to catch Mo's attention. "I'll take a bottle of Pinot Grigio," she said, enunciating clearly so everyone could hear her over the karaoke disaster.

If not for the noise coming over the speakers, she suspected she would have heard twelve people simultaneously inhale. At a time like this, it was hard to remember these people were her friends. That she'd sat at church with some of them on Sunday mornings. That they'd banded together just a few months ago to help a family in the village get through a bad time.

Maybe that community spurt of love and generosity was a one-time thing. Maybe all the stars had aligned that one day, and it would never happen again.

Mo handed her the bottle, his eyebrows slightly raised.

She clasped the chilly bottle. "Take it off my paycheck."

As she walked away, he called, "I will. And it's not cheap."

"Neither am I," she shouted back, just as the karaoke stopped. She had a fleeting glance of bulging eyeballs and dropped jaws before she headed into the back.

She'd come into the place on the verge of tears, and she was leaving on the verge of laughter.

One thing she could say about her life was that it

wasn't boring.

––––––––––––––

Mo watched her stride away with her chin up and shoulders back, like the queen he'd called her earlier. Holding the bottle like a scepter.

Buzzing started behind him. Someone called his name and asked how Rosa was doing, and he told them as far as he knew, she was doing as okay as anyone could when their husband was an asshole.

That drew laughter and more requests for drinks while they put down Mike. The karaoke started again, someone on the small stage who didn't sound as if she was being strangled, and the drinks flowed. He made small talk and smiled a lot. Lisa and Brenda were smiling, too. Tips were always good on Saturdays.

By two, he figured he'd worked a good fourteen hours, and his feet hurt. He'd turned thirty-nine last October but felt older as the last bunch of customers straggled out with loud goodbyes, the designated driver bellowing that no one better barf in his car.

Twenty minutes later, Mo locked up and headed upstairs.

His door was open. The light was on.

He stopped in the hallway. In Jersey, he'd be hauling ass out of there and calling a cop.

But the village of Miracle, Wisconsin, was closer to Dorothy's Oz than Jersey...and he could think of only one person who would be in it.

He stepped into the lighted apartment.

No one was in the living room.

No one was in the kitchen.

No one was in the bathroom.

The bedroom light was on.

On his bed, Rosa lay on her back, breathing softly, looking like Sleeping Beauty, even in baggy comfortable pants and a black T-shirt that said MO'S in big white letters. But he sure the hell didn't feel like the prince who woke Beauty with one kiss. He felt more like the frazzled Papa Bear coming home to find Goldilocks in his bed.

Maybe he was dreaming. Only, if he were dreaming, his feet wouldn't still hurt, he wouldn't feel tired to the bone, he wouldn't smell like grease and garlic and burgers.

He bent and nudged her. She moaned, and it reminded him of the kind of moan a woman made during sex. Though it had been so long since he had any that pretty much anything an attractive woman said made him think about sex. That went double with Rosa. All she had to do was breathe for him to imagine her naked and saying, *Take me, Mo. Take me now.*

She was his middle-aged sex dream.

He nudged her again. She moaned again, and his body responded. Proving he possessed one body part that still had some energy left.

Her eyes opened. She smiled at him sleepily. "Mo! I've been waiting for you."

The scent of wine wafted to his nostrils. He sat up. "How much wine did you drink?"

"Just a couple glasses." She pushed up on her elbows.

"What size glasses?"

The sleepy softness left her face, her muscles clenching. "I didn't use measuring cups. The bottle is in your fridge if you want to check it."

He held her gaze for a second and saw the awareness in her eyes. His body relaxed. "I don't need to check anything."

"Good." The tension visibly eased out of her. "I didn't

come here to argue with you."

He sat on the edge of the bed. It felt good to get off his feet. "You wanted to reenact the story of Goldilocks and the Three Bears?"

Her smile was slow and sensual. "I don't have gold locks, and I've never seen you as a bear."

"I won't ask you what animal you see me as."

She laughed, a sound of enjoyment that hit his happy spot. "A kitten."

He groaned, and she laughed louder. "Okay, not a kitten. A leopard. Sleek and fast and deadly."

"Now I know you're lying. I'm more like one of the workhorses in an old-time circus. Doing a dozen things and then trotting in a circle while people ride me."

Her eyebrows lifted, and he realized his voice had turned hard. He shook his head. "I don't know where that came from."

"Me?" She scrabbled back from him.

He ignored the urge to reach out and touch her. "Not you." He peered down at his hands. They looked like the hands of a much older man. A working man's hands. A man who got things done.

He wasn't the horse that trotted in a circle, after all. He was the draft horse that pulled the circus train.

She bent her knees and wrapped her arms around her legs, holding them to her chest. "I came in to get the sheets you said I could borrow. I couldn't find them, so I thought I'd just take a nap and wait for you to come up."

"The sheets are in your room."

"Along with the Christmas decorations." She grinned.

He managed a smile. This was part of his dream coming true. Rosa in his bed. But she was wearing too many clothes and saying too many words.

But why not on the couch? Why fall asleep in his bed?

"I tried sleeping on your couch," she said, as if reading his mind, "but it was lumpy. And the bed in your second bedroom doesn't have sheets either. Just the cover. I didn't think you'd mind if I napped here."

"I don't mind. The singing downstairs didn't bother you?" he asked, trying to put the wishful thoughts out of his mind—though when he was around Rosa, that was like trying to stop breathing.

"I enjoyed it."

"You like torturing yourself?"

She laughed again. Not light and happy but dark and husky. A warm, liquid laugh that slid into his blood and through his veins. A bedroom laugh that wasn't letting him forget they were in his bedroom, sitting on his bed. That it was late at night. That she was the woman he'd dreamed of ever since he'd come to this village and seen her walking down the street with her hips swaying and her head up. And he'd wondered who she was.

And that's the day he'd gone into the Amber Waves of Grain, found out it was for sale, and three weeks later, he'd changed the sign to Mo's place.

"I like being in your bed." Her head tilted and her full lips curved up

"What pie did Sam bring you?" he asked to change the subject and stop him from saying how much he liked her in his bed. Or saying it would be much better if he and she were both in bed together.

But he couldn't do that. He was her boss and her friend. He wasn't going to do anything that would change that.

Besides, he was curious about Katie Guthrie's pie. He'd heard about them his first week in Miracle. How she often baked one pie, gave it a name, and dropped it off at a villager's house. The pie name always pertained to something the villager was going through.

He didn't buy the magic part. It was easy enough for Katie to know what was happening in the village. To know who needed comfort, who needed encouragement, who needed a Go To Hell Pie after a bad break-up.

But this village, with the belief that a miracle was prophesied, had built her pies into something more than they were—which was damn good.

"Sam said it was a Get Lucky Pie," Rosa said.

He went still. "And did you?"

"With Sam?" She grinned.

He didn't realize how rigid his body went until the tension eased out.

"He's a friend. We don't see each other like that."

"He may be a friend, but he's a man, too. Any man…any straight man…sees you like that."

Her husky laughter spilled out again. She could put it on sex tapes and make a pile of money.

"You're good for my ego." Her head tilted. "You asked the wrong question." She looked at him with a small smile. Waiting.

Like a good poker player, he flattened his lips, keeping his face blank and his mouth shut.

"You didn't ask me if I wanted to get lucky." She waited another two seconds before her lips opened again. "The answer is yes."

He swallowed.

She smiled. "And you didn't ask who I wanted to get lucky with."

Unable to glance away, he stared at her as if she mesmerized him. So much for his poker face. This man-woman thing had always been harder for him than any card game.

"You shouldn't go there," he said.

"You keep warning me off." Her forehead creased. "Am I reading the signs wrong? You don't want me?"

"Don't make me say it."

She sucked her lips in, her face fearful. Hurt.

He caved. He was a lousy liar anyway. "You've been drinking." He put his hand up. "Yeah, I know you're not drunk, but even a couple drinks can lower our inhibitions and make something stupid sound irresistible. When—*if*—we do make love, I don't want either of us to be sorry the next day."

"You're right." She put her head down, her hand on her forehead. Took a deep breath. Her breasts lifting then lowering under the big white letters of his name.

A groan came out of his mouth. Her head lifted, and she stared at his face, as if trying to see into his mind.

She smiled slowly. "You *do* want me."

"I told you I did. And I don't lie."

"You're a man. Men lie."

"Not me." He shrugged. "Not when it matters."

"You would lie to keep from hurting my feelings."

"Even if I wanted to sleep with you—"

"And you do." Her tone was firm, her back straight, her eyes bright.

"I'm tired. I might be lousy."

"I was married for twenty-six years. I'm used to lousy sex."

He laughed. This woman... She was everything he needed. Everything he wanted. She was a joy to all his senses.

But he shook his head again. "I've had some...setbacks."

"Who hasn't?"

"My life's been torn apart."

Her face, filled with teasing and fun like any teenage

girl talking to a teenage boy, turned sober. She scrambled up then sat on the backs of her legs. "Do you want to talk about it?"

"Let's keep to one difficult subject at a time."

"Difficult." She put her hands to her cheeks and shook her head. "Katie's pie was way off tonight."

"If I did what you want, I'd be the one who got lucky. And that's the problem." He shrugged. "I'm not used to being lucky."

Her lips closed and so did her expression.

He turned toward the hall. "It's been a long day and I smell."

She didn't reply, but he heard the creak of the bed as she got up. "I like the way you smell." Her voice sounded different. Softer. Smaller.

Someone who was hurting.

He turned and grabbed her upper arm. She looked back at him, her eyebrows up.

"Sleep in my bed tonight," he said.

"Alone?" Her mouth screwed up, her eyes narrowed. The expression of a woman about to tell him to drop dead.

"Not alone. With me. We'll sleep in the same bed together. Just sleep."

She stared at him for a long moment, the tension like a taut string between. "You're sure?"

"Are you backing out?"

Her lips curved and lifted; her eyes glowed. Her skin glowed, too, as if bathed in moonlight. "When I say I do something, I do it."

He nodded. "I'll take my bath."

"I'll get my PJs."

Alarm shot through him. "What you're wearing is fine."

"I don't sleep with a bra." Her breath huffed. "What are you afraid of?"

"You. Don't put on anything too sexy."

As she left the room, she laughed again. That's not what usually happened after he asked a woman to sleep with him, but he'd take it. If Rosa was in the mix, he'd take anything.

17

When he returned to the bedroom, she was stretched out on her back, on the side closest to the wall. In winter, he usually slept in a pair of boxers and a T-shirt. In summer, he slept commando. He had the towel wrapped around his hips, his upper body cold. He should've been smart enough to bring the underwear into the bathroom. But Rosa had shaken him up.

He didn't turn the bedroom lights on, not wanting to wake her. The hall light spilling into the bedroom was enough to see by. He tossed a T-shirt onto his shoulder then rummaged through his underwear drawer, finally finding a pair of boxers.

When he closed the drawer, he looked at the bed and saw her on her side, facing him, her eyes open.

As he headed to the bathroom to change, he almost expected her to call out something like, *You may as well stay. You don't have anything I haven't seen before.*

She said nothing, but he felt her eyes on his back until he closed the bathroom door.

This was a bad idea.

He returned a minute later and dropped his clothes on a chair near the door. She lay on her back now, her head turned toward him, her eyes so dark they looked black. He turned off the hall light and crossed to the bed, careful of the dresser. This was not the time he wanted to stub a toe or do something stupid.

Then he lay next to her. Smelling her. Hearing her breaths. Not touching her but feeling her warmth. Her proximity just inches away. Feeling her gaze on him even in the dark.

Instead of her proximity making him tense, it felt...good. All of it. Even the desire that roiled in his stomach and below his stomach. Even that felt good.

"It's nice to be like this," she murmured.

"Yes," he said. He felt like he was under a sensuous spell. He was a poor sailor on the sea. She was Lorelei, singing a tune to lure him into the depths of the ocean, where he would never be seen again.

But what a way to go.

The bed creaked and the mattress dipped as she turned and shifted closer. Her length touched his, her breasts under the cotton T-shirt pressed against his upper arm, soft and warm and supple.

"I'm not asking you to make love to me," she said. "But can you just hold me? It's been a long time since a man held me in bed."

He looked at her. His eyes weren't yet adjusted to the darkness, but he could see a blacker shape in the lighter blackness. "You could have any man in the village."

She laughed low. "Not true. And I don't want any man. I just want you."

"To hold you."

It took her a couple seconds to reply. "Just that."

He turned. She was asking him to do what he yearned for. "You want to spoon?" he asked.

"No." She shifted closer to him, her body pressing against his. "Just hug me," she whispered. "Hug me tight."

Feeling like a pimply kid with the prom queen, he held her as she lowered her face onto his neck and held him just as tightly. As if they were hanging on to keep from falling apart.

Finally her grip loosened, and so did his. His eyes

closed. His body loosened. He smiled.

"It's nice just sleeping with someone," she said.

He sighed in reply, because it felt as if his world that had shifted so many times in the last few years had taken another change. And this one was good. So good. So good. So good...

So temporary...

But just for tonight, he would hold her and be content.

———————

Even with the shades pulled down, the early morning light filled the bedroom with its golden softness. Barefoot, Rosa stood at the end of the bed and enjoyed the sight of Mo sleeping, one arm swung out to the spot where she'd lain a few minutes ago. His face looked younger with the tension smoothed out by sleep. At peace instead of always moving, always thinking of the next job to do.

If he were her husband—which of course would never happen—she wouldn't give him a to-do list. Instead she would find his list, grab a thick pen, and start crossing chores out.

Once in a while, he needed to just sit and breathe. He needed someone to help him do that. Someone who would show him how to enjoy life.

But it wouldn't be her job. She didn't come here to fix him. Right now she was too injured. Her spirit bruised. Not because of Mike. She just wanted that over so she could go on to the next part of her life.

But Nick... He'd treated her like the enemy, and it was a wound to her heart.

Sucking in air, she tried to push away the gathering despair. It resisted her willpower, clinging to the corners of her mind like wet mud. She looked at Mo sleeping, taking in his clear forehead, the bump on his nose, the way his hair sprung up from his head, the firmness of his chin, and then his wiry, muscled arms.

She had to hold back a groan, but the mud slid away, and her body relaxed with a rush of heat. She stepped back, took one last look at Mo sleeping, then left the room and headed down the hall. Away from Mo. Away from temptation.

What was she thinking of last night? God, she was so pathetic, forcing him to sleep with her.

At least he'd turned down her even more pathetic attempt to have sex with him.

She reached the kitchen. Seeing a pad of notepaper with the trademark of a winery and a salesman's name, she grabbed it and sat down to write him a thank you note.

Mo, she started. And immediately got stuck. Something about putting it all on paper was scary.

Thank you for...

She moaned. For what? Sleeping with her? For not having sex with her?

No. She really didn't want to thank him for that. She had wanted to make love to him, and sleeping with him was not the same thing. It was second best.

Why lie? It wasn't the sex as much as feeling like a desired woman again.

And she knew Mo desired her.

And she desired him. She had the feeling that sex with him would be good. *Very* good.

Katie's pie hadn't been wrong. She was lucky he let her move into the apartment upstairs. Lucky he let her sleep in his bed. Lucky that she fell asleep while he was holding her.

Still, she would've liked a little more luck.

A little more Mo.

Maybe another time.

Or maybe not.

The sun streamed into the kitchen window, and she raised her face upward to soak it in, the rays giving her strength. Making her feel like the kind of woman who expected to be treated with seriousness. The kind who didn't thank a man for not sleeping with her.

Feeling less needy, she looked down, ripped the top page off, and crumpled it. She started again.

I enjoyed sleeping with you. The only problem is we were slightly overdressed. Next time we spend the night together...

She tore it off. Crumpled it.

That wasn't right either. He would laugh. Shake his head. Think it was a joke.

This indecision wasn't like her. She had always been a take-charge woman. The one who made sure everything was done.

At Fabrini's, she'd been Mo's equivalent. The queen bee.

Now she was just a worker bee.

She wasn't sorry. Though she sometimes had to fight her inclination to take charge and get things done—because getting things done was in her DNA—she kind of liked being the worker bee. The one who went upstairs with a bottle of wine before the restaurant closed. The one who slept in her boss's bed. The one who acted the vamp.

Not a successful vamp. She was too straightforward. She was like the zebra trying to be a giraffe. It just wasn't possible to grow that long, skinny neck. Wasn't possible to be what she wasn't.

She took a deep breath. She knew what needed to be done now. What her zebra self could do without trying to change her stripes into spots.

Dear Mo,
Will you be my fuck buddy?
Respectfully,
Rosa

Her pulse throbbing, her head light, she looked down at her words. Nodded. Let go of the pen. Pushed up from the chair though her knees didn't want to go anywhere...and then walked out.

The next move was up to him.

18

Mo stared at the note. The words were written with large loops. Pure Rosa.

He got coffee. Sat down. And he stared at the note some more.

Finally he got up and went into the hall, passed the other apartment's closed door, and headed downstairs. The newspaper wasn't there, which was unusual since he'd woken up later than usual this Sunday morning.

He headed back to his room. Never mind the newspaper. His own reading material had to be more interesting than the news. He poured another coffee then sat down and stared at the note again.

A tap came at his door. It could only be one person. Without asking who it was, he opened the door and saw Rosa holding a bag that said Wegner's. She wore a pale pink sweatshirt with a saying on it that he couldn't read without staring at her breasts. Considering her note, that wouldn't be a smart thing to do.

Though it might be a fun thing. And it wasn't as if he often had fun.

"Good morning," she said. "You're frowning. Aren't you happy to see me?"

"I'll think about it and give you the answer when I find it."

"When you find it? Like lost keys?"

"Like lost common sense."

Her eyes lit up, and she beamed at him. She seemed younger and slimmer than when they first met. Going through hell could thin down a person. But he liked

Rosa's curves and wouldn't want her to lose any more. To him, she was perfect before, and she was perfect now.

"Are you talking about me or you?" she asked.

"You go too fast for me. I'm having a hard time keeping up with you."

"I don't believe that." She held up the bag. "Mind if I use your fridge? I cleaned the other one then plugged it in, but it's not working."

He stepped back to let her inside and watched her walk to his kitchen. Her swaying hips could hypnotize him. It felt to him as if everything was leading her to his place. To him. Pushing them together. Even the electrical appliances.

She put the bag on the table. He left the hall door open and strode to the kitchen.

"Your refrigerator is practically empty." She loaded it with eggs, almond milk, apples, cheese, and bread, her movements quick, the way she did everything.

"I eat most of my meals downstairs."

"Then I guess you wouldn't want to eat this." She held up a Kringle, a Danish pastry with a pecan filling.

He reached for it. "You're guessing wrong. I'll cut it."

She started to say something, and the trill of her cell phone from her apartment stopped her, the sound traveling down the hallway and into his place. He saw the tension in her face as she stared over his shoulder, the smile in her wiped out.

"I should get that." Her voice flat, she set the Kringle on the table then stepped toward the hall.

He grabbed her wrist, and she swung her gaze to him, her forehead creased. "Let it ring," he said.

Her mouth opened then closed. She nodded but stood with her face tense until the phone stopped ringing. Only then did she shiver as if her tight muscles were loosening. He crossed to the hall door and shut it so more rings wouldn't bother her.

When he turned back, she was cutting the Kringle as if nothing had happened. "Plates?" she asked as he approached her, giving him a determined smile that didn't match her shadowed eyes.

He touched her cheek, and she closed her eyes and inhaled. They remained like that for a few seconds until he moved away from her and her eyes opened.

"I normally use napkins," he said. "But for you I'll get plates out. And coffee."

"I feel honored." Her voice had a wobble. "A real plate. But a napkin will do." She reached to his napkin holder that looked like a pizza. A gift from a vendor. Nothing like pizza décor to class up his apartment.

When he returned with two coffees, she was sitting with her hands folded on the tabletop, the Kringle by her unpainted fingernails, her eyes on the note she'd written.

She raised her gaze to him, and he felt the intensity of her emotions, though she didn't say one word. Just took the warm mug from him. Sipped the coffee. Took a bite of the Kringle, chewing for a long time as if making it last.

He devoured his in three bites. Then took a couple gulps of his coffee before setting the mug down.

There was a dead silence between them. Back in Jersey, he'd been in a lot of poker games, and this reminded him of the ones with the high stakes.

He was reaching for another piece of Kringle when she spoke.

"You read the note."

He drew back his empty hand and looked sideways at her. "It was hard to miss."

"Any response?"

His fingers tapped the table. "From my body or from my mind?"

The corners of her lips tilted up. "Your mind. I already know about your body."

"I have something in my past that keeps me from...intimacy."

Her gaze flickered down to his lap, her forehead crimping, her mouth open in a cross between horror and sympathy.

"Not physical," he said quickly, and her quick laugh made him scowl, and then the relief on her face made him grin.

"Men are so sensitive." Her lips curled into a smirk.

"Not like women."

"Not in *that* area."

He nodded. "No argument there."

"So..." She leaned toward him. "There are two answers to my question. Yes. Or no. But you gave me an excuse."

"I'm married."

Her expression closed up like a jail door slamming shut. She sat back in her chair, pulling her hands off the table as if it were contaminated. He could practically see a sign light up on her forehead, saying *NO FUCKING.*

Then she inhaled deeply, her nostrils spreading, and her rod-straight body curved into the chair. She reached out and touched his arm.

He looked down. He wanted this badly. Too badly. Once upon a time, he'd had everything he wanted. Now the things he most wanted were the things he couldn't have.

"Your wife isn't with you," she said. "Is your separation temporary?"

He stood. She deserved an answer. But not here. He'd

have a hard time getting through it. A hard time doing the right thing by her. The kitchen was too close to the bedroom. And she was too beautiful, too sensual, too everything. He wanted to do the right thing, but he'd never claimed to be a saint.

"Let's go for a walk. I need fresh air."

"Cold air." She made a face but stood. "I'll get my coat and gloves."

They met in the hall, and her expression was subdued. He guessed she'd listened to the message on her cell phone, but she didn't say anything and he didn't ask.

"Life is messy," he said.

Her laugh was sharp as she led the way down the stairs in her long black coat, with a dark red hat and scarf. He wore a black knit cap and a Packers jacket he'd bought to blend in with the natives. No one looking at him would suspect he was a Jersey boy.

It was in the forties outside. The forecasters with their snow warnings had been way off. It was practically balmy out, the snow melting on the grass. This early on a Sunday, there wasn't much traffic. The services at the two churches had probably started already. And probably a few of his customers from last night were sitting on pews praying that their heads would stop pounding.

Not everyone, though; a car slowed, and Madeline Schilling, a minion of Linda Wegner's, gawked at them, her jaw dropped. Rosa waved, and he stuck his gloved hands in his pockets.

"This was a bad idea," he said. "People will talk about us."

"You think they're not talking already?" She gestured widely. "By now, everyone in the village probably knows I'm staying in your extra apartment. Half the people no doubt already believe we're sleeping together."

"What about the other half?"

"The other half thinks you're in the closet."

"Gay?" He heard the disbelief in his voice as they passed Miracle Taxidermy and Reupholstery.

"They speculate that's why you were kicked out of the Mafia and are on the run from them."

If there had been a chair nearby, he would've plopped down on it and stared at her. Instead he kept walking, feeling as if she'd hit him on the head with one of his wine bottles.

"The Mafia? How the hell did anyone connect me to the Mafia?"

"Your accent. Like on TV and the movies."

"You people need a life. The Mafia is everywhere, not just in New Jersey."

"Not Miracle." Her eyebrows rose. "Unless the speculation about you is true."

"No." Hell no. And that was the truth. But not the whole truth. Just to know that people connected him to the Mafia made him think of putting a For Sale sign on Mo's Place. Rumors spread fast, and they spread far. Even a small village like Miracle had Internet. Hell, even his restaurant was on the Internet.

But no pictures of him were included. And no one who knew him in Jersey would look at the pictures of his restaurant, bar, and karaoke stage and believe he had settled for this tiny nowhere village and this third-class restaurant. It was too different from his old supper club, a place where Sinatra and his Rat Pack would've felt right at home. That wasn't the Vince Moretti they knew who greeted his diners like they were old friends or family. And often they were both—Family with a capital F.

They reached a corner, and she turned left, away from

Main Street.

"What do you think about the speculation?" he asked, the warning buzz in his mind on low now but still there. He glanced at her profile—her sharp nose clearly Italian and so were her full, curving lips—and the warning buzz didn't matter.

He had it bad.

She wanted to be his fuck buddy. No strings. No attachments.

Not on her side. But he felt as if a string attached him to her, the way a dog collar and leash attached a dog to a human.

He held back a harsh laugh. It would be too easy to be her dog.

"I knew you were straight," she said, stopping his thoughts. "I could tell the first time we met. The way you looked at me." She glanced sideways at him, her eyes bright. "As if you wanted to take me on the nearest table and make mad love."

"You were with Mike then."

"I'm not with Mike anymore."

"You're still married."

"Not in my heart." She tapped her gloved fist over her left breast.

"You were married in the Catholic church, weren't you?"

"What about it?" She shot him a dark look, her eyebrows slashing down.

"They won't recognize the divorce."

"I don't recognize their non-recognition." Her eyebrows lowered farther, her eyes darker, her jaw jutted out. "After we split up, my former maid of honor, who lives in Ohio now, called to let me know she and Mike were having an affair during our engagement. That he and she continued it after I was pregnant with Matt, and it only stopped when she found out he was seeing another woman." She held out her gloved hands, as if to God. "How can I trust a man like that?"

"You can't."

"You." She stopped and he did, too. "I think I can trust you."

A big chunk of frozen unhappiness inside his chest melted. He hadn't even realized it was there, keeping him from feeling bad, but also keeping him from feeling happy.

Without it, he felt his chest and lungs stretching. Opening. And he could almost see a dark cloud spiral out of his mouth and nose. Overpowered by the relief, his vocal chords clenched together, and he stood there on the sidewalk, inhaling and exhaling noisily.

"Are you okay?" she asked.

Nodding, he straightened, his breaths slowing until his throat opened and he could talk. "I had to leave my family. I can't tell you why."

Her mouth opened, but he shook his head, stopping her as he went on. "My wife refused to leave with me. Her family is...very Catholic. They consider marriage to be sacred. She told me she would never divorce me."

She started to reach up then pulled her hand back and glanced around. Checking to see if anyone was watching them. But no cars drove along the side street. No one else was out walking, though a dog barked down the block, and another bark answered, then another.

"How long has it been?" she asked, returning her attention to him.

"More than three years. I don't want to say any more."

With a nod, she turned toward Main Street. "Let's go

back."

As they walked, he hunched his shoulder against a cold gust in his face. They reached Main Street and headed toward his place. The wind slanted against the side of his face, not giving him any relief.

"So now you see why we can't have a love affair," he said.

"I didn't ask for love," she said. "I said 'fuck buddy.'"

His heart beat fast. Though another wind gust hit him, his body heated.

"So, what do you say?" she asked.

"I say we should walk faster."

19

Tony waited for Rosa. Her second child. Leaning against the restaurant's side door that was the entrance to the two apartments. His arms crossed, he scowled as he watched her and Mo hurry down the main sidewalk toward the bar.

Rosa's stomach knotted. Mo moved a couple inches away from her, but that just made him look guilty. Besides, it was a waste of time. If any of her sons could tell when two people were in heat, it was Tony. He was the most primal. The hunter, fisher, gatherer. Matt, her oldest was the artist, creating masterpieces with food. And Nick...he was the emotional one. The one who carried the most hurt inside him. The one who'd made her feel the most hurt.

She turned onto the narrower walk that led to the side door. Mo lagged behind so she could go first to meet her son.

Tony straightened away from the door and stepped down to the sidewalk. No scowl on his face now, but no expression either.

She didn't walk fast.

Tony's lips twisted, and he lowered his head and shook it. And then his lips stretched into a big grin. The same as when he was a boy playing tricks on her. All these years later he still loved his pranks.

Not nearly as much as she loved her son.

She ran the last few steps, right into him. He gave her a bear hug before releasing her.

"Hey, Mo." He waved to Mo with his bare hand, and

she opened her mouth to tell him to wear gloves today. Before any words came out, she snapped her mouth shut. He would just tell her he didn't need them. Her tough guy with the tough skin who some days made her so mad.

And this day he made her so happy, because he was here for her.

She reached up for another hug and a kiss on his cold cheek before stepping back again and beaming at him.

"Hey, Tony," Mo said behind her. "Let's go inside so you two can talk."

They clambered up the steps, Tony leaving a couple clumps of snow on the treads. At the top, she opened the door to her apartment then stopped in the entrance.

"Holy shit, Mom. This is a mess." He glanced at the hall where Rosa stood. Mo had gone on to his apartment, and in her peripheral, she could see Mo slip inside.

"I know."

"You can find a better place to stay."

"Where? Who? And the important question." She held up her hand and made the money gesture. "How much?"

Instead of answering right away, he rubbed the start of a mustache over his top lip, as though it held the clue to the secret of the world.

If he knew that secret, she wanted him to tell her. She'd been searching for it since October when she found out about Mike's wandering penis.

She unbuttoned her coat. "Let's go inside. I'll take your jacket."

"I can't stay. I have to be at work this afternoon." He worked at a hunting and fishing store near a lake in Wausau, about forty-five minutes from Miracle. He and his friend were planning to buy it from his friend's uncle.

Tony had big plans. In addition to the store, he wanted to be a hunting and fishing guide. All things outdoors. When he'd quit Fabrini's, Rosa had seen the change in him. As if he'd gotten hold of a Get-Out-of-Jail-Free card.

She wished she'd known a long time ago how he felt about working in the restaurant. She would have found a way to help him.

And she wished she'd known a long time ago that Mike was cheating. She would have divorced him long ago. Kicked him out before he made her look like a fool. She'd suspected a few times, but he always lulled her fears.

Stupid, stupid, stupid. She couldn't believe how stupid she'd been.

"Hey, Mom. You okay?"

"Fine. I'm fine." She took off her coat, while Tony walked around the apartment. When he reached the bedroom with no sheets, just the bedspread, she winced.

He would know. Even though she and Mo hadn't done anything, he would still know.

"Why are you staying in this dump?" he asked.

"I left suddenly and knew it was empty."

"So it's just temporary?"

"That's what I planned, but I think I might stay after the house is sold." She winced. "Once my lawyer straightens things out, I can clean the place up and make it look good. And the price is right."

He scrubbed his hand over his mouth and chin. "You're paying for Matt's college fees, aren't you?"

She frowned. "Why do I feel like I'm being interrogated?"

"Dad's an asshole."

"I won't argue about that."

He laughed, and it came out angry.

"Your father and I agreed that since the house was paid off, I'd take care of Matt's costs. Mike was paying for the apartment with Amber and said he couldn't afford it."

"Now he can."

"He *can*." She grimaced and gave him her good-luck-with-that look.

"Yeah, I doubt it, too. If he refuses, let me know. I'll tell Nick."

Hope sprang up inside her. She would have her baby back again. She stepped toward Tony, putting out her arms to hug—

"'Course, that little shit will stay with him anyway."

She gaped at him. Feeling ill.

"Aw, Mom. You know he doesn't really give a crap about the eyes of the church. It's all about the money and the restaurant. When I quit, he practically did a victory dance. He wants it all, and he sees this is the way to get it."

"No." She shook her head. "No."

"Ah, shit, Mom." He looked at her with pity in his eyes. "Matt and I suspect Nick's the one behind Amber admitting the baby is her ex-boyfriend's. I bet Nick made her miserable, and she figured Dad's money wasn't worth it."

She looked down at her black shoes, seeing them through a film of unshed tears. Her eyes burned, but her skin chilled. But she wasn't going to cry in front of Tony. He didn't need to see her weak like his.

Sucking in air and mucus, and blinking away hot tears, she raised her head. "It's okay." She nodded at him. "I'm going to be okay."

"I know you're going to be okay. And don't worry, I'll

talk to the little shit. I'll let him know what I think of him."

"Honey, just—"

"Hey, it's not your fault. He takes after Dad. It's genetics. Matt and I take after you." He shrugged. "Nothing you can do about it."

"He's still my son."

"Yeah, but I'm your favorite."

She laughed too loud and too long, until he looked at her with pity again.

Stopping in mid laugh, she pulled herself up as tall as she could. "You are my favorite. But don't tell Matt."

"Nah. I'll just tell Nick." He pointed behind him at the bedroom. "Doesn't look like you slept there last night."

"The mattress felt damp. Mo let me sleep on his couch."

"If you slept with him, you don't have to lie to me. It's okay to have revenge sex."

"Tony! Maybe it's okay, but we didn't have it." Her voice rose with every word.

He held up his hands in surrender. "Okay, okay. Just sayin', if you change your mind..." He shrugged.

"You wouldn't mind?"

"I like Mo. He's an okay guy. Pretty much everyone who works for him defected from Dad's place."

She nodded. She'd noticed that.

"They all have good things to say about him. They say he takes care of them. I know he loaned Scotty money to get his car fixed when it broke last winter. And Lisa said when she went on vacation and someone stole her purse, he sent her money."

A good feeling started inside her, easing the hurt. She held back a proud smile. As if he were her boyfriend or her lover. When he was...just a friend. That was all.

"And I saw the way he looked at you a few times. I think he's younger, but you look good for your age."

She laughed and shook her head. A compliment and an insult at the same time.

"So if you like him and he makes you happy, go for it. You deserve to be happy."

Her laughter stopped, and tears gathered in her eyes again. This time she didn't try to stop them. She reached up and hugged Tony. "You really, truly are my favorite."

He hugged her once then stepped back. "I better go now or I'll be late." He strode toward the hall. "I'll call after I talk to Nick."

He clomped down the stairs, and she waited for the sound of the closing door before she headed to Mo's apartment. The door opened before she got there. Mo stood in the entranceway.

"What did he say?" he asked.

"He gave me permission to have an affair with you."

He looked at her for a long moment then shook his head. "Miracle is the strangest place I ever lived in."

She took two steps toward him with her arms out. "Just shut up and make love to me."

20

"You have time before your bar opens?" Rosa's normally rich voice quivered.

Mo closed the door behind her. She wasn't the only one who was nervous. He felt like a kid again, which was normally a good thing. But not when he was about to have sex with a beautiful woman. A woman who he'd taken one look at and his heart felt like it grew too big for his chest.

The lower parts of his body had grown, too.

"More than enough time," he said.

"I hope that means more than five minutes."

He laughed until he noticed she wasn't laughing, her eyebrows down and her mouth pensive.

"You're serious?"

"Serious as if the oven in your restaurant kitchen stopped working."

"I guess the performance bar for good sex isn't high."

Laughter sparked in her eyes. "Do you need that bar low?"

He grinned, and the heaviness he'd carried with him every day for the last three years lightened. "Is that a challenge?"

She laughed. "Are you up for it?"

"I've been ready since the minute you told me to shut up and make love to you."

A frown crossed her forehead, and her smile wobbled, a flash of unease on her face. Just for one second, and then she smiled brilliantly. But her eyes...they lowered, avoiding his gaze.

He gestured to the couch in the living area, the joy slipping away. "Just talking is fine. We have a few hours. There's no need to rush into the bedroom. We don't have to do anything now or ever..."

She put her hands over her face. "No, no, you have it wrong. That's not it. I'm being too bossy."

The joy surged back. He held up his hands to the ceiling in an Italian gesture that meant from my lips to God's ears. "I love bossy women."

Her face opened into a grin. "No one likes bossy women. Even I don't. Bossy men, either."

She turned from him and stepped into the living area. It was a small room that overlooked Main Street. She gazed at his brown leather couch and leather recliner as if she were seeing his apartment for the first time.

He looked, too, trying to see his place through her eyes. Wondering what it said about him. The floor was wooden and old, and he'd stained and oiled it. He'd left the flaws in because they added authenticity. It gave him a sense of solidity. This place had survived a lot, and so had he.

There was a bookcase on two walls and a forty-inch TV he didn't have much time to watch. He'd always been a doer, not a watcher. But right now he was content to watch her in her black slacks and red sweater. Tall and shapely and emotional, with something that pulled him to her every time he saw her. Even when she and Mike had still been together. When he'd found out they'd split up, he'd smiled all day, everyone asking him if he won a lottery.

But, no, it was just that for so long it felt as if all happiness had been shut off to him... As if God looked down at him from heaven and shook his head and said, "Not you. No special reason. You didn't do anything wrong. But someone has to have bad things happen, and I chose you. That's just the way it goes."

As if for years life had been a dark cloud...

And that day a ray of light had broken through.

A ray of hope.

She crossed to the front window and looked down at Main Street. He came up next to her and looked down, too, content to not rush her. This wasn't a normal seduction with dinner and wine and knowing what was going to happen.

This wasn't a seduction at all. Just sex.

"We need a build-up," he said.

"Really?" Her expression looked doubtful, and she peered down at the front of his pants.

"Not me." He fought the impulse to hover his hand over his zipper. "That's not what I meant."

Shrugging, she raised her gaze to his face. "I thought you were a little young for Viagra. Unless you meant a hand job or a blow job."

His face was growing warm. "I wasn't talking about that, either. For the first time, let's just..."

"Fuck," she said.

Laughter bubbled up inside him, and he wasn't the bubbling kind of guy. Her earthiness was one of the things he most enjoyed about her. "The way you say it, 'fuck' is the most beautiful word I've ever heard."

"It's a good word. If you weren't talking about your penis, what kind of build up did you mean?"

"Romance. Slow music. Slow dancing. Wine, if you like."

"Wine might make me sleepy," she said.

"Then we'll skip that."

"Let's skip the music, too." She put her hand on his arm. "I like to dance. I danced two weeks ago. But sex...I haven't had sex for five months."

He breathed easier. "I can take care of that."

"I haven't had *good* sex for, um, five or six years."

"Now you're upping the pressure again."

She laughed until she pressed her hand on her stomach and her eyes gleamed with moisture. He felt happiness pouring off her and thought, *I'm going to make her happier.*

Making her laugh—making her happy for even a short time—made him feel...better. Good.

He didn't love her. How could he? It would be futile to love any woman. Heartbreaking.

But his body could love her. Cherish her. Satisfy her.

He put his arms around her shoulders. Her laughter stopped, and she gazed into his eyes as if trying to read his thoughts. He stared back at her beautiful face with the strong bones and full mouth and eyes the same color as his favorite dark chocolate ganache cake.

"I feel like a kid," he said. "As if it's the first time."

She groaned. "I hope not. The first time wasn't that great for me."

He remembered his first time clearly. Not that great for his fifteen-year-old girlfriend...but for him it had felt like he had won the Daytona 500 on foot. The best thing he'd experienced in his entire fifteen years.

"My first time wasn't my best performance, either," he said.

Worry touched her forehead again, lines appearing.

"Are you backing out?" he asked. "If you don't want to make love, we don't have to. Or we can take it slow. Sit on the couch and cuddle."

"I don't back out." She stood straighter. "We can do it really fast. If it's not good, we can at least get the nervous part done with. The next time we'll be better."

He caressed her cheek, feeling the smoothness of her skin, admiring her eyes, her nose, her lips, her chin. She could make a poet out of him.

"She walks in beauty," he murmured. Then he grinned. "And she talks like a nervous teenager."

She slugged his arm. He grinned and stepped back.

She smiled, and he could see the change in her. Reclaiming her usual confidence. She turned toward his bedroom first, but he stepped quickly after her.

Looking at him, she said, "Let's make love."

He started to reach out to her when a thought hit him. "I don't have any condoms."

Her smile disappeared, her eyebrows raised. "I sure don't."

He stared at her, and she stared at him. Then her smile came back.

"There isn't much chance that I'll get pregnant. And I don't have any STD's or any problems."

"Me neither."

"Then what are we waiting for?" She held out her hand. "Let's make love."

21

She stood on the wooden floor in front of the foot of the bed in her bare feet. His kiss was gentle, yet it scared her. Electrified her. Made her cling to him and press against him.

Her shoes and socks were the only items she managed to remove before his arms came around her. He was taking over.

She liked it. And she didn't like it.

She wasn't used to letting go, letting someone else take care of her.

He held her back. "You're stiff."

"So are you," she said.

He laughed, but his eyes...they looked into hers with sadness. "We don't have to do this."

"No." She shook her head. "It will get better. Just go ahead."

His mouth curved into a shape that wasn't a smile or a frown but a little of each. "This is a bed, not a dentist's chair. I wasn't planning on pulling a tooth."

"It's not you, it's me."

"Oh Christ." He dropped his arms and stepped back.

"No, no, I'm..." She held out her hands. "I'm scared."

"I wasn't planning on hurting you."

She put the heel of her hand to her forehead. Now she was offending him. This was going from bad to worse and then worse yet.

Her dating experiences when she was younger had never been this clumsy. She had smiled and flirted, and the boys had done everything she wanted, like puppies eager to please.

So she had married Mike, who didn't do everything she pleased. She'd thought he was manlier. More confident.

Over the years, she realized he was just more selfish.

And now here was Mo, a man with real confidence, trying to make her feel good. She knew he was the grown-up version of the best of the young men she'd known. But she wasn't a teenage girl, so supremely confident of her allure. She'd been hurt. Humiliated. She'd lost control of her life.

She was...damaged.

He pressed his lips together, lowered his gaze from her eyes to the doorway, then turned and started toward it.

No! She could fix this.

She held out her hands. "Let me please you."

His gaze shifted back. His body still turned away.

She took a step toward him and another and yet another, until she stood so close to him that she could feel a hum shiver through her body, a slight current. A reaction she'd felt before with her skin so close to his.

"Do you feel that buzz between us?" She pitched her voice low and smooth.

He faced her, watching her as if she were a snake at an Indian bazaar, uncurling upward. "I've felt that buzz since the first time I saw you. And every time after that, even the times you were standing next to Mike."

"Let's not mention his name. Not now." She curved her hand on his, feeling the warmth of his skin. It was easy to imagine that his whole body felt this warm.

And her body felt cold. So cold. As cold as she imagined the real hell was. As cold as her heart.

"I'm happy to forget about him," he said.

She nodded, looking into his brown eyes and seeing a man who would never hurt her. Though that wasn't true. She'd seen enough of life to know that people hurt other people every day. Usually without thinking. God knew she was guilty of that.

He wore a thick blue shirt, and she reached up and opened the first button, keeping her gaze on his face. On his eyes.

He kept his gaze on her eyes, too, not blinking as she unbuttoned the other buttons. Until finally his shirt hung open. Then she stepped back. The T-shirt beneath the shirt advertised one of the beers he sold downstairs, though she'd never seen him drink beer.

"Now what?" he asked.

A shiver passed through her. He was asking her. She was in charge of this.

Warmth kindled inside her, and the only tension in her body now was sexual tension. "Now you can take off the shirt and your T-shirt."

A breath later, the shirt was tossed on the chair by the entrance. His T-shirt was next.

She laughed and heard the breathiness. Not anything like her usual laugh. She didn't feel like her usual self at all, and she liked it.

"Now what?" His eyes laughed at her, and the hum whispering on her skin grew louder.

"Your pants. They need to come off, too."

He glanced down. "Okay if I take my shoes off first?"

"You don't have to ask my permission. You can do anything you want."

He stared at her for seconds, and fear pricked the warmth, the happiness. Fear that he would ask what game they were playing. And she would have no answer except "life."

Then he sat on the bed and took off one shoe and then the other.

The fear drifted away, and relief washed over her. She closed her eyes. How quickly the insecurities had come back. That wasn't who she was, and she didn't like that woman. Her marriage to Mike had changed her. She'd been like a shiny box that hadn't been treated well. She'd gotten tarnished and nicked.

She didn't want to be damaged anymore.

Her eyes snapped open, and she watched Mo undress. His movements swift, he stood in front of her seconds later in glorious nudity. He could have been a statue, created by a master sculptor. He had the thin, wiry body of a man who kept in shape through constant movement for most of the day. A runner's body, with a flat stomach and muscles in his arms and calves. Not much fat on him.

And his erection was...very nice. Standing up at a slight angle to point at her, as if saying, *There you are. Come closer, baby, and we'll have a good time.*

She laughed at her imagination and moved closer.

"My body is funny?" he asked.

"Your body is fabulous." She touched his neck first then his shoulder. Her lips against his skin, tasting the saltiness and the warmth.

Already she felt the nicked parts of her healing. The tarnish sliding off.

His breathing quickened. His arm curved around her back and tugged her to him. A sound came out of her throat. Wordless. She melted against him like she was butter and he was a warm muffin.

With a tilt of her head, their parted lips met. She sighed into his mouth, and the kiss deepened.

It felt as if she'd been waiting for this kiss her whole

life.

She could kiss like this for hours.

Yet only a moment passed before she realized she wanted more. She wanted to feel his warm skin against her cooler skin, not against her clothes.

She pulled away from his kiss. "I think I'm overdressed."

As she grabbed the hem of her top, it was his turn to give a low-pitched laugh that waltzed atop her nerve endings.

After all, making love was like a dance. Some people did it well. Others did it like amateurs. She and Mo weren't lovers. They were potential dance partners.

Unlike Mo, who dropped his clothes on the floor, she folded each piece carefully, putting it on a blue chair near the door. With just her red panties on, she faced him. Aware of his gaze on her, she stood straight and proud, only holding her stomach in a little.

His gaze warmed every spot it traveled over. It felt as if he touched every inch of her but her hidden places. She could feel the folds between her legs swell. Feel the juices flow. Her nerves wakening. Preparing for his touch. His entry. Eager for it.

Still watching him, she finally took off her panties. He smiled widely and opened his arms. A small sob came out of her mouth as she slid into his arms, and she didn't know why that sob came, except this must be the way pure happiness made her respond. The surprise and wonder working on all her emotional systems.

They fell into bed kissing, her breasts against his chest, his erection against her belly. Her wonder intensified, and so did the desire. She pushed away from him then and rained kisses on his body, started at his chin then going down, down, down. Telling him between kisses and nibbles and licks how wonderful she found his body. How she loved the feel, the smell, the taste of him.

Until he groaned and pulled her up and turned her onto her back and said, "My turn."

She laughed and heard the exultation in it. Heard the joy and the power.

And then he started kissing and nibbling and sucking. Her breath hitched, and unlike her, he didn't talk. There was only the hum of the furnace running and her little noises she couldn't hold back. Until all she could hear was herself saying, "Oh, oh, oh, oh, oh."

And then his head was between her legs, and she screamed, "Oh, oh, oh oh, oh, oh. Aaaaaah!"

And then he raised his head and his wonderful, brilliant tongue from between her legs. He slid up over her and kissed her deeply while she throbbed for him and moaned and throbbed some more.

And then he pushed in. She clenched herself around him, and more screams came from her. It was as if her body had been waiting for this joy for years, getting little tastes of what could be, but it was never enough. Never reaching fruition.

And now she had it all. The whole meal—appetizer, main dish, and dessert. Her body was feasting on it. Reveling in it.

She could do this forever.

And then he tightened and grunted and held himself up with his arms stiff, and he lifted his head while he pulsed inside her. He stayed like that for seconds. His body shook. The cords in his neck and biceps stuck out. Then a strangled sound, almost a sob, came from his throat. Still pulsing, he lowered himself until he lay on top of her.

She wrapped her arms around him, and her body

relaxed, as if it were giving a satisfied sigh. And she thought maybe they couldn't do this forever.

But later, they could do it again.

22

Dario,

Just another note to tell you how much I love you. Something good happened to me today, and I feel happy. Yet there's still a piece of my heart missing, and that's you.

It's coming on to Valentine's Day. You're probably too old to get a Valentine's Day gift from your mom. You probably have a girlfriend. You were always a good-looking boy. You got the best of your mom and me. I can't send you anything except love. And I do that every day. Send you love. And every day I pray for you. Your mom, too.

I wish...

The buzzer rang, the timer, telling Mo that he needed to go downstairs and get to work. He would finish it later. He'd written it by hand today instead of turning on his computer. He didn't want to be distracted by the electronic world, taken away from this world and this apartment.

But now the time had come to leave.

It had been a short morning.

The shower stopped. He stuffed the unfinished letter in the newspaper then set it on the table by the sofa. Only then did he cross to the bathroom, knock on the closed door, and call Rosa's name. Smelling lavender and imagining her—

She opened the door. Holding the towel in one hand.

Standing tall and naked, water drops on her pale olive skin that had felt like satin under his hands. Her breasts were full and spectacular. Her hips a perfect curve.

"You're torturing me," he said and heard the rasp in his voice.

Her laughter was low. "You can have all this later."

"Promise?"

"Of course. We're fuck bud—"

"No." He held out his hand, the humor gone. "We're not any kind of buddies."

"Then what are we?"

"Lovers." Before she could say anything, he left. The picture of her naked body, dropped jaw, and wide eyes imprinted in his mind.

He ran down the stairs feeling like a teenage boy who'd gotten lucky, grinning all the way.

Mo had told Rosa before she showered to make herself at home, so even though he was gone, she stayed after the shower. His place was sunnier and cleaner than hers. She didn't like to sit on the furniture in her apartment. Everything looked forty years old and smelled funky. And since she didn't plan on staying once her lawyer sorted Mike out, she didn't want to buy new furniture.

She made herself coffee then served herself a piece of Katie's Get Lucky Pie.

Once again, Katie's pie magic had nailed the occasion.

This one was creamy caramel-apple pie. When she finished the piece, she licked the plate. After all, no one was around to see her.

She debated getting another piece but decided a second piece might lead to a third one. She had a lover now to impress with her figure. She would save the next piece for this evening after work. She and Mo could both have one, since they'd both gotten lucky.

This was her day off, but she would go downstairs and mingle later, if only to watch Mo. Her lover. Discreetly, of course. She didn't want to shout it to the village.

In the living room, she caught sight of the newspaper. It was sure to have something sad that would take her mind away from the pie that still called to her, saying, *Eat me, eat me.*

As she picked up the newspaper, a sheet of paper fell from the inside. She grabbed the sheet, and it unfolded as she lifted it up. Wondering if it were something she should throw away, she glanced at the paper and recognized Mo's slanted writing. The salutation had the name Dario. Wondering who he was, she started reading it.

She gasped then slapped her hand over her open mouth. *Oh no. Oh no. Oh no.*

Dario must be his son. Mo had mentioned his son and his wife, but they were just spoken words then. They hadn't seemed real. But now reality crashed into her mind, and so did the questions.

Why was Mo separated from Dario? Why couldn't he see him?

Was it the mother? Was he on the run from the police? Or was Linda Wegner right, and he really was a former Mafia member?

Her mind rejected that. It was too crazy.

And the "something good happened" that Mo said had happened to him... That was her. *She* was the something good.

She couldn't even be pleased, too shocked by the knowledge that Mo was separated from his son. And to be apart from him for years...

She thought of Nick. It would be unbearable if they were never together again. If this...disconnect between them lasted for years.

Tears burned her eyes, and she grabbed a napkin. Tears wouldn't help Mo. They wouldn't help her, either.

She wished there was something she could do. She wanted to snoop and find out more. But Mo was a smart man. He could handle his life. And for sure he wouldn't want to be helped. No man did, unless it was something to do with laundry or cleaning or making appointments.

Then she remembered that Mo wasn't most men.

She curled her knees up to her chest, an ache in her heart, wishing there was something she could do to help him.

23

For the next few days, Mo had to remind himself to scowl occasionally. To look bored and grumpy. To complain about the weather and taxes.

The two premier gossips in the village, Linda Wegner and Angie Schuster, the village beauty shop owner, could smell happiness like a bloodhound smelled a raccoon. When they did, it would take them less than a minute to put two and two together and guess that he and Rosa were together.

For Rosa's sake, he would hate it. Not for his sake. He wanted to shout it, to sing it. To paint a sign for the whole village to see.

Before this, he'd sometimes thought God had sent him to Miracle so Rosa could taunt and torture him. As if He'd made her just for him...then fixed it so he wasn't able to touch her. This woman who had the hips and legs and breasts of his perfect woman. And her beautiful face. A strong face to fit a strong woman. In mind and in character. A woman who did the right thing. As beautiful inside as outside.

And she could cook. Italian food! A woman who was a walking temptation to men like him. She had skin like—

"Hey, Mo."

Sitting in his office chair downstairs, he started. He'd come downstairs to order supplies and instead had thought about Rosa.

He turned in his wheeled chair to see Katie Guthrie, who was delivering pies for the day.

"You caught me daydreaming," he said. He'd gotten a

delivery from his meat guy earlier and had left the back door unlocked for Katie.

She grinned. "I wonder what you're daydreaming about."

He narrowed his eyes at her. Since she'd brought over her Get Lucky Pie for Rosa, he was pretty sure she guessed what his daydream was. But she and Rosa were good friends, and she wasn't a gossip.

He supposed someone who sometimes got up in the morning knowing what pie to make and the person she should deliver it to had learned circumspection.

Not that he believed in her magical pie powers. She was just...intuitive.

"Need help bringing in the pies?" He got to his feet.

"Nope. They're in the kitchen. I have something else for you."

"A special pie?" he asked. She'd never brought him one before.

She shook her head. "Something else. Just a sec. I'll bring it here."

"You want help?"

"Not yet. Wait here. It's a surprise. I'll be right back." She hurried out of his office, a tall woman in her late twenties who used to look a little lost. But since her videographer fiancé had moved in with her, she'd blossomed.

He knew what that felt like. Someday he was going to wake up and see rose petals falling out of his ears.

As he started for the hallway, he heard Katie return, her steps hurrying. Since she'd been insistent as well as mysterious, he waited. Trying to guess what she was bringing. A cake? As if during the night, a cake fairy had visited her and whispered that she should start a cake line to go with her—

117

She rushed into his office, holding a cat carrier.

A piteous meow went right through him.

And it came with an echo.

She set it on the floor about three feet from him.

He stayed where he was. "What is it?"

"Kitties. Wanna see?" She crouched and unhitched the little gate. She peered up at him. "You should close the office door, or they'll get out."

He obeyed her, wondering how it was that he had kittens in his office and he was letting his formerly meek pie baker order him around. It wouldn't happen in Jersey.

Of course, he didn't have Rosa in Jersey.

She would fit right in, too. The men would love her. The women would respect her...and be jealous because their men wouldn't be able to keep their eyes off of her.

As soon as he shut the door, Katie stood, the carrier gate open. She stepped back.

Another piteous cry with an echo came from the carrier. She crouched again, about a foot from the opening, her hands flat on the carpet, her face level with the carrier door. "Come out, sweeties. No one will hurt you." Her coaxing voice was pitched higher than usual. She peered up at Mo. "They're afraid. It's been hard for them. They almost froze."

He closed his eyes. He'd seen enough between the blue plastic bars to know they were two gray and white cats on the small size. He didn't want to look closer and see their little cute faces. He didn't want to hear their sob story.

But he may as well try to stop a tornado. She stood and threw her hands out, gesturing as if Italian blood ran through her veins.

"My dad found the mom and the two kittens in the

barn this morning. We never saw the mom before. My dad has an arrangement with the vet. When he sees new strays, he brings them in and the vet will spay or neuter them."

Mo nodded. He could guess the payback arrangements her dad and the vet had made. He'd been in Miracle for only a couple of months when he learned about the special crop that Sam Guthrie grew in his cornfield.

"When he brought the mom in, the vet found she'd been microchipped. Dr. Leolin contacted the owner, who said her cat had been missing for seven months. She picked it up but didn't want the kittens." Katie made a face. "Dr. Leolin said the Humane Society has so many cats now they're offering a two-for-one deal. I can't take them. Gabe and I are renovating the kitchen and it's a mess. Dad doesn't want indoor cats. I thought maybe you could keep them here and—"

The sound of footsteps coming down the stairway from upstairs stopped her. Mo straightened. Rosa.

Her name sang in his mind. *Rosa, Rosa, Rosa.*

"Katie," she called from the hall. She must've seen Katie's van in the back.

Katie opened the hall door and stuck her head out. "I'm here."

"With another pie?"

"No, something else. And I don't think Mo likes it."

"I like cats," he said, and heard the defensive note in his voice. "But I've never had them as pets, and there's a health code here and—"

"I know, I know." Katie pulled her head back into the office and rolled her eyes at him. "The health code."

"I'm not making this up. I have nothing against cats."

"They don't need to be downstairs. You can leave the

food, water, and litter box upstairs, and they'll be fine."

Rosa entered the room, saving him from sounding like a kitten hater. "What something else? Oooh." She caught sight of the carrier, and her face softened the way women's faces did seeing babies, puppies, and kittens. Especially kittens.

He had a sinking feeling in his gut.

"You're adopting kittens?" She gave Mo the same soft look.

"No." He shook his head emphatically. "Hell, no."

"You don't like kittens?" Her eyebrows contracted, the soft look replaced by a frown. One second a hero, the next a bum.

"I like kittens," he said.

"But he's never had one," Katie said.

"I didn't say that."

"I can tell."

As he wondered what that meant, she turned her back on him and told Rosa the story of the mother cat and the vet, and then she came to the place she'd left off.

"So Gabe made a video of the kittens and put it on YouTube." She shifted to include Mo in the conversation. "I thought Mo would show them on the TV in the bar. Gabe said you can get the Internet on it."

"I can, but I never use it. I wouldn't know how."

"Ask Scotty. If he can't do it, call us, and either Gabe or I will drive over. If anyone's interested in the kittens, you can take them upstairs to see the cats."

"Lisa's working tonight," Rosa said. "She had two cats. I'm sure she'll tell everyone about them."

"I'm sure she will, too." Mo adjusted his thinking. It was smarter to give in than to be known as the kitten hater. "Sure, glad to do it."

A mewl caught his attention. He looked down. A gray

and white kitten was rubbing its head on his shoe.

"The kitty likes you," Katie said with a squeak of surprise.

He crouched and put his hand out. "Of course it likes me. They can tell when someone is safe." He lowered his voice. "Isn't that right, Checkers?"

"Checkers?" Rosa gave him an approving smile.

The things men did for women, he thought. Then a soft, fur-covered head rubbed against his hand, and he felt a burst of pleasure. He picked it up and cuddled it. "Aren't you sweet? A real cutie pie."

"Do you know what you just said?" Katie asked, her eyebrows way up, a half smile on her face.

"I called it 'sweetheart.'" Now what had he done wrong?

"No. You said 'cutie pie.'" She laughed at him. "And you know me. I always bring the right pie to the right person."

He stared at her, still holding the kitten and wondering how to wiggle out of this. Before he could say anything, she and Rosa both burst into laughter. Katie pointed at him. "You should see your face."

"Thank you." He nodded at them. "I'm delighted to entertain you."

"You never cease to entertain me," Rosa said. "That's why we love you."

He stared at Rosa, his heart pounding and his breath stopped.

The kitten squirmed in his arms as Katie headed to the doorway. "I'll get the litter box and cat food. Be right back."

The door closed behind her, and Rosa picked up the second kitten, "Look! This one likes me." Her face glowed with pure love. The mostly gray kitten rested its head on her breast, as if it were coming home.

Mo set down his kitten, and it started to play with his shoelace. He stared down at the gray and white fluffy animal batting its paws at his shoe.

Unlike Katie, Mo never claimed to have magic in any field. Certainly not cats. But the sinking feeling that still remained in his gut told him where these kittens would end up.

"I always wanted a cat." Rosa's voice was dreamy. "Or even a dog. We almost got a cat last spring, but it ran away. Mike doesn't like cats, and I think it could tell." She rubbed the kitten under its chin. "You are a beauty, aren't you?"

The sinking feeling in his gut sank lower.

_____

Snow started about six that night, though the weather forecasters had predicted the snow would stay north.

Wrong again.

At seven, their last diner left, the snow coming down pretty hard, and the forecasters were predicting five to eight inches. Mo sent everyone home, then it was just him and Rosa. And two kittens.

"We have to bring them upstairs," she said, following him to the office where they'd left the kittens. Mo had known everyone would want to run back and coo over them. He'd hoped someone would want to take them home, but so far no takers. Maybe a different day when the snow wasn't keeping his usual customers away.

"We can put them in your apartment," he said.

"We can't leave them alone."

"They won't be alone." Even as he said it, he knew it was futile. "They'll be together."

Silence came from behind him. "That's all right," she

said. "I understand."

He turned around. "Understand what?"

"You don't want the kittens." She spread her hands. "I'm just staying here temporarily, and I'm not going to force you to do anything you don't want to do."

The stubbornness swooshed out of him, leaving him sad and deflated. Wondering why he was being so adamant about the kittens. They were cute and playful, and when she left, at least they would be entertaining. They would keep him from feeling sorry for himself.

Not that he planned to have them stay with him. By then someone should adopt them.

"We'll bring them up to our place," he said.

Her eyes jerked up and grew wide. He turned before she could ask when his apartment had become *our place*.

24

"Five inches of new snow on Main Street are like diamonds on a woman's neck." Mo peered out of the front window of his apartment. "The buildings across the street look like they belong on a calendar."

Rosa came up behind him, holding a kitten against her upper chest. "It does hide the shabbiness," she said. Under the early-morning sun, the snow sparkled. By her house, the trees and the space would look like a fairyland.

Only she wasn't living in it anymore, looking out at it.

The thought didn't give her a pang of envy. Just sadness when she thought of Nick inside the house with Mike. She didn't care about Mike. But Nick...

The kitten woke with a sudden wiggle, and she kissed the top of its head. Katie had said the kittens were about seven weeks old, and there had been a couple accidents already this morning. Checkers had used a plant as a litter box, and the one in her arms had left a puddle on the bedspread.

Mo hadn't said anything. Just had the long-suffering man look on his face, but he stripped the bedspread and the sheet and put them in the washer without saying anything.

It would be easy for a woman to fall in love with a man like that.

He was a wonderful lover.

A good cook.

A great boss.

And now he cleaned up after kitten upsets.

A dangerous combination for a woman like her.

"What's the latest weather?" she asked. She'd been on the computer, looking up techniques on teaching kittens how to use the litter box. The consensus was that they were fastidious animals and would learn soon. But she wanted them to learn *now*. Especially after she'd caught Checkers sniffing one of her shoes.

Her shoes were *not* litter boxes.

She petted the kitten's tiny neck, and its wiggles changed into purrs while it kneaded her shoulder with its front paws.

"More snow," Mo said. "The forecaster says five to eight inches."

She groaned.

He glanced at her, his eyes warm. Smiling.

Because of her, she thought. That's why he was smiling.

Her heart squeezed. Right now, she felt like she was in a Hallmark movie, cast as the heroine. The story was about a woman who always knew the way home...and one day the home disappeared.

So she had to find a new home.

Only this wasn't her home. And it really wasn't his either.

He had a son in New Jersey.

And a wife. Mustn't forget her, even if the wife hadn't left with Mo.

A white van parked in front of the bar. Tony stepped out of it, and she felt Mo's tension.

"You're going." His forehead creased. "Sure you don't want to wait for the lawyer?"

"Tony wants to be there with me when I pick up my stuff. We'll be back soon."

"If you come back," he said.

She stared at him. Was he...worried? "I'm not living with him again. He cheated, and I don't respect him."

His expression was sober. "I'm a cheater, too."

"So am I. But it's not the same thing." She squared her shoulders and raised her chin. When she spoke again, she heard pride ringing in her voice. "Are we supposed to let them reject us and say it's okay? Be miserable for the rest of our lives? Or go back to someone we no longer respect and don't even like?" She flung out the hand that wasn't holding the kitten.

His eyes burned the way they did in the bedroom. He took a step toward her. "You're—"

The doorbell rang, stopping Mo and jarring Rosa into a breathless laugh. She lifted the now sleeping kitten off her shoulder and handed her to Mo. With a sleepy protest, it settled into Mo's arms. "That's him. I have to go now."

She started to turn.

"Wait," he said. "A kiss before you go."

"I'm coming back," she said, making her voice firm.

"I know." Despite his words and smile, she saw doubt in his face.

She leaned forward and kissed him hard and fast, then swirled around and hurried to the hall door, grabbing her coat and gloves from the chair near the doorway.

She had to leave fast before she told him the real reason she was coming back.

It wasn't anything to do with Mike. It was everything to do with Mo.

But right now both their lives were in limbo, like a satellite halfway between earth and the sun with only three choices: crash to earth, get burned by the sun, or keep orbiting.

———————————

Holding the kitty, Mo watched her get into the van.

"Good luck," he said, his voice low.

The kitten murmured sleepily.

The van drove off, and Mo kissed the top of the kitten's head just because it made him feel better.

"There goes my heart." Rubbing the kitten's neck, he added, "She said she'll come back, and you better pray she does, or you'll have to leave."

As if she understood, the kitten lifted her head and gave a piteous yowl that twisted Mo's gut.

Mo kissed the kitten's head again, and it immediately purred.

He had the sinking feeling he was in trouble.

———————————

"You came to your senses," Mike said.

He looked...fatter. Standing in the front foyer—because Tony's garage door opener hadn't worked, which meant Mike had changed the code—Rosa recalled that stress made Mike eat.

She gave a mental shrug. Not her problem. He'd been stocky these last few years but still handsome in a ruddy way. But she could tell him that the waitresses weren't likely to be attracted to a chubby boss. Not even the bimbos.

Only she wouldn't. She didn't care, and Nick was here since the schools were having a snow day. Nick would care that she said something like that. Care that she insulted his father.

She wasn't questioning Nick's motives. He was still her son. He hurt her, but it didn't stop her from loving him. And it didn't stop the hurt.

"I'm not coming back," she said in reply to Mike's question. Why did everyone think that? They should know her better. "I'm here for my mother's rosewood desk, the Madonna my uncle painted, and my grandmother's china."

He braced his legs. "I don't think you should take anything out of the house until the lawyers work it out."

"She won't take anything out." Tony braced his legs. "I'll take it out for her. How are you going to stop me?"

Mike gave him his disapproving glare before turning to Rosa. As if his disdain would make Tony fall in line. Even though Rosa had told him a thousand times over the years that his disapproval didn't work with Tony. It just made Tony more stubborn.

Tony was her rebel child, and she had always understood him better than Mike did. Somewhere inside her was a rebel child, too. And at five years away from fifty, she was finally letting it loose to play.

"There's gossip going around about you and your boss," Mike said.

"Really?" She shrugged one shoulder. "How...ironic."

His face flushed. "It's easy to put two and two together. You're living above his bar."

"In my own apartment. And it's a restaurant."

"They sing karaoke!"

"They eat my lasagna. And they *love* it."

He opened his mouth, and she held up her hand, staring straight at Nick. He stood behind his father. His father's wingman. Stiff and wooden-faced. His eyes not quite meeting hers.

"How are you, honey?"

"He's fine," Mike said. "He's doing really good living with me."

"I heard you bought him a new car," Tony said.

"What?" Rosa snapped her gaze to Nick, whose face was turning the color of her spaghetti sauce. Whose gaze still wouldn't meet hers.

"He deserved it." His mouth set like an angry bulldog, Mike glared at Tony. "For staying with me when my other sons deserted me."

"Dad, you're a—"

"Tony!" She gripped his forearm. "Don't say it."

"I'm not saying anything that isn't true."

"We're not playing truth or dare. Let it go for now." She gave him her pleading look, which she used rarely. She'd rather command than plead. Her voice low, she said, "We don't have to stoop to his standards."

He shook his head, his mouth tight. "If someone fights dirty, we should fight dirty back."

She let go of his arm. "We win by not fighting dirty. We win by being the better person." She shifted her gaze to Mike. "Now, get out of my way so I can collect my stuff."

"I can't let you do that." He glared at her. "It's not in the papers you signed."

"In the papers I signed, I was living here."

"You could still live here instead of at that bartender's."

"Since you didn't sign your set of papers, I think that voids anything I signed. But if you don't want me to take items from my family, I'm just going to make a phone call."

She took out her cell and opened the directory. It was there somewhere in the middle.

"Calling Jerry again, are you?"

"Not this time." She pressed a number to dial and looked up at him. "I'm calling Linda Wegner."

The red flooded back into his face, and his hand

snaked out to grab her wrist.

Tony gave his arm a karate chop.

Mike yelped, his arm dropping. Rosa stepped back, her heart pumping hard, her breaths fast. She hadn't thought it would get ugly.

She'd overestimated Mike's decency. It wasn't the first time.

Her finger shaking, she turned on the speakerphone button.

Tony glared at Nick. "What do you think of your father now?"

Nick's lower lip wobbled, his eyes wild. A wordless sound of half sob, half rage came from his mouth, then he snapped around and ran toward the back hall.

Tony sneered. "Coward," he said, loud enough for Nick to hear.

"Rosa." Linda's voice had an excited squeak that sounded amplified in the foyer. "I'm so glad you called. I heard you and Tony drove to Mike's and your house. Are you moving back with him?"

"Hello, Linda. No, I'm at my house to collect a few things I left. You remember my mom's rosewood desk."

"Of course. She loved that desk."

Rosa nodded. Linda got a bad rap in Miracle for her gossip. But she wasn't actually malicious. She shared good things as happily as gossip that could hurt people. She had a gift for gossip, and when people had gifts, well, Rosa thought they should use them.

"And the Madonna painting by my grandfather?" she asked. The door leading to the garage slammed, and Rosa clenched her teeth against a twist of pain in her chest.

"Oh boy, how could I forget that? My grandmother dated your grandfather, and he gave her a Madonna—but it wasn't as good as the one he did for your grandmother." Her voice turned dark. "After she died, my Uncle Mark took it. My mother still hasn't forgiven him."

"And my grandmother's china?"

"I can't forget that, either. My grandmother bought a set just like it. We always thought she was jealous of your grandmother. Why are you asking these questions?"

The garage door opened, and Rosa flinched. "I'm at—"

"Stop." The glare Mike gave her blazed with hate. "Take it. Take it all, damn it."

"Oops. Never mind, I have to go."

"It's Mike, isn't it?" Linda asked. "He's not letting you take them, right?"

"Sorry, I really have to go. Bye." She hung up.

Mike's glare blazed hotter. "Why, you bi—"

"Dad." Tony's voice was sharp as he stepped up to his father, his face inches away. "You call Mom a name, I'm going to slug you."

Mike glared from her to him then he turned and stormed away.

Rosa was shaking. She wished she would have stayed with Mo today, played with the kittens. Played with the man. Wished she was anywhere but here.

"Let's get the desk first," Tony said.

She walked forward, her steps wooden, and wondered when it was going to get better.

25

"How'd the meeting with your lawyer go?" Mo asked on the other end of the prep table, cutting lemons like it mattered. But the only thing that mattered was that Rosa would soon return to her house. The only thing that mattered was how much more time she would stay with him.

Three weeks. He'd had that much time with her already. He'd known from the start that it was temporary and told himself he was lucky to have that much.

She shrugged one shoulder. "She has a great tan and looked glowing."

"I wonder who has the balls to marry a divorce lawyer," Scotty said, stopping by the table. "I'd be more scared to marry her than if I were a rabbit surrounded by starving, feral cats."

"He's a lawyer, too," she said.

"Figures. Rich get rich. Lawyers get lawyers."

"What about cooks?"

"Cooks get laid." He winked at Mo, a leer on his face. Then his expression changed to horror. "Shit, I didn't mean that, Rosa. Sorry I said anything."

As he strode away, his earlobes pink, Mo glanced at Rosa to see if she looked hurt. Instead she leaned into him and whispered, "Yes, we do. And we get laid very well."

His whole body heated. Three weeks with her. The best three weeks of his life. Every night, he went over the day and night, imprinting the memories, the stolen looks, the smiles, the kisses, the lovemaking. Even the two of them playing with the kittens and the way her jars and tubes took up most his bathroom counter, leaving him only a small square.

He stored the memories like they were precious. When she moved back to her house, he wanted to remember it all.

He'd learned before how easy it was not to notice the small things. Sometimes even the big things. So when Theresa had looked at him with coolness that last day, as if she wouldn't be sorry to see him go, as if he'd been a necessary nuisance in her life for the last few years, he hadn't blamed her. It had been his own fault. If he'd paid her the attention he'd paid to the restaurant, she might have had a few tears and regrets.

And for him... His sadness was for Dario. Not her.

This time he was paying attention. In these last three weeks, he'd lived more fully than ever in his life.

But now the lawyer was back.

He looked down at the lemon.

Damn lawyers. He never did like them.

He tried to smile, but his lips wouldn't listen to his brain. Rosa frowned at him, seeing right through him. No faking it with her.

"What did she say about the house?" he asked.

Her frown deepened. "What about the house?"

"About getting Mike out so you can move back in."

"Oh." She leaned back and crossed her arms, as if protecting herself. "Since Nick is staying with his father, I decided to let them have the house until it's sold. My lawyer's going after him to pay for Matt's school and expenses instead. And if he wants to keep the restaurant, I still get all the money for the house."

He clenched his teeth to keep from shouting out his profound relief.

She was still his. At least for a while longer.

"I asked her to have his finances investigated. It's clear that he's been lying all this time. He bought a car for Nick."

"He could be paying for it in installments."

"If you knew how cheap he was..." Her lips twisted, her eyes narrowing. "Or maybe he was just cheap with me. Spending his money on his girlfriends. If that was the case, I definitely want to know."

He didn't reply. He'd heard the gossip about Mike. In Miracle, it wasn't true that everyone knew everything. Not the wife. And maybe not the kids, though from Tony's anger at his father, Mo suspected he'd known along with everyone else.

"Do you want your rooms back?" She looked down and to the side, as if avoiding his gaze. "I can find another place to stay."

"Don't," he said.

"Don't what?" She raised her eyes and looked straight into his.

He reached out and took her hand in his. "Don't leave."

They stared at each other, no words, their eyes saying it all.

A cough made him jerk his hand from hers. At the same instant, she jumped back.

Laughter came from behind him, and he recognized Lisa's laugh.

Rosa stared behind him.

More footsteps came from the other side, Scotty returning.

"Honestly," Lisa said, "do you actually think everyone in the village doesn't know about you two in your love nest?"

"Linda Wegner probably knew the second you two first went to bed together." Scotty snickered.

But Mo wasn't laughing, and as far as he could see, neither was Rosa. She was staring at the two as if they'd turned into aliens.

"I think she has spy cams planted in every room of every house," Lisa said. "How else can she know so much?"

"She's a witch." Scotty grinned.

"No one said anything to me." Rosa's voice was weak. Disbelieving.

Mo shook his head. She'd lived in the village her whole life. She should know the quirks and social behavior of the inhabitants.

And from what Mo had observed, there were plenty of quirks, though the social behavior was more likely to be social *mis*behavior.

"Not to you," Lisa said. "You *know* Linda doesn't tell the people involved. That would take the fun out of talking behind their backs."

"Ouch," Scotty said. "You've been a Linda victim?"

"You mean you haven't?" Her back curved, and she leaned forward to stare at the fly of his pants. "Oh, now I understand your omission."

"Real funny."

She punched him in the arm and sashayed away. Scotty snorted and headed the opposite way.

"You think the whole village knows we're having an affair?" Rosa asked.

Not affair. Living together. Mo held back the words in his mind. The only thing they kept in the other apartment was Rosa's desk and some of her clothes. She'd insisted on hanging the Madonna in his living room on a wall that didn't have any pictures. Besides

Rosa, it was the most beautiful thing in the place.

Though he admitted the kittens were entertaining, making him laugh as they dashed around the place in a frenzy. And when they fell asleep, hugging each other, even he felt warm and fuzzy. Though their puking... It was a good thing for them that they were so cute and he owned an industrial carpet cleaner.

"You know what this means?" he asked.

Her forehead puckered, and she shook her head.

"It means we don't have to pretend." He picked up a towel and wiped his hands. He stepped closer to her, curved his hands around her shoulders, and drew her to him. His mouth inches from hers, he said, "It means we can do this without worrying that people will see."

And then he kissed her.

———————————

One second Mo told her something that had her gasping. The next he was kissing her like they were lovers in a movie, her spine curved back, him holding her with an arm around her shoulders and the other around her waist.

He used tongue.

Anyone could see them.

She made a small kitten sound. Everything inside her soared. Her heart, her joy, her heat.

She wanted him. More than ever. A tide of want.

Right now.

She couldn't wait.

But not here. Not where anyone walking by could see them.

She put her hands on his shoulders and used the heels of her hands to push him away. It didn't work. He was further gone than her. Holding her too tightly. Not letting her go. Not taking his lips from hers. And she knew—she knew, she knew, she knew—that he needed her as much as she needed him.

As if he had to have her soon or something inside him would curl up and die.

As if he needed her more than he needed air.

As if they were twin souls separated.

As if—

One last shove and he released her.

Immediately she missed him. Immediately she wanted him back. Wanted all of him.

Someone was talking to Scotty and Lisa in the back. A male voice she didn't recognize. Good. Maybe they wouldn't notice when she and Mo disappeared upstairs for twenty minutes.

She held out her hand, but Mo didn't take it.

He looked...odd. As if he couldn't take it all in. His eyebrows indented.

Her hand dropped. She knew he wanted her. She couldn't believe that had changed in a second.

The voice in the back was louder. His head tilted, and he turned toward the back.

"Mo?" she asked, hearing the smallness of her voice. The uncertainty.

He looked at her, and in his face she saw pain and wonder and fear.

And then he turned away again and took a step toward the back.

And then the door to the back opened, and a man burst through.

No, not a man. A boy-man, about five ten or eleven and skinny, with soft lips and eyes that were dark chocolate brown.

He stopped in the kitchen. Stared at Mo who was

standing like a statue. And his eyes, the same chocolate brown, glittered with tears.

Rosa put her hand to her chest and gasped. Looking from one face with a firm jaw to the younger one with the same firm jaw.

"Dario." Tears welled up in Mo's eyes, too. His hands out, he stepped toward his son.

"Dad!" The man/boy barreled toward Mo. They met and clutched each other. Mo, who was the most solid man Rosa knew, started to sob, even as he repeated his son's name, over and over. Dario sobbed, too. Tears ran down his handsome face, his face scrunched.

Rosa remembered Mo's unfinished letter, and her eyes prickled. Mo had written that Dario was his sun and his stars.

Now he had his sun and stars back.

She scrubbed away a tear trailing downward then turned toward the break room, which led to the back staircase to the apartments.

Once again everything was changed, and she had packing to do.

26

Mo glanced around but couldn't see Rosa. She must have left to give him and Dario private time. That was like her. Everything good and wonderful was like her.

It was like Dario, too.

He clasped Dario's shoulders. He didn't want to let go of him. As if he feared his son was a figment of his imagination and would disappear if he stopped touching him.

"How did you find me? What are you doing here? Jesus, I missed you so much."

"Me too." Dario glanced to the side, the same skitterish look the kittens had when faced with something new.

Mo glanced sideways to see Scotty and Lisa watching. Lisa was holding a cup of coffee and staring, as if she were watching a movie.

"Don't you two have work to do?" he asked.

"Sure." Lisa didn't move right way. Instead she grinned at Dario. "You're cute. He's really your dad?"

"Hey!" Mo said, the happiness inside of him making him want to laugh. "He's too young for you."

"He's still cute." Lisa winked at Dario.

Tears still glittered in Dario's eyes, his lips spread into a goofy smile. Mo knew he had the same smile on his face, the same tears in his eyes.

"Hey, kid," Scotty said. "Glad to meet you. Your dad's a good boss." He flapped his thumb toward the upstairs. "We're not open for another ten minutes. You want privacy, better go upstairs."

"Scotty and I should be able to handle everything," Lisa added. "And Rosa. If it gets crazy, we'll call you."

"Come on." Keeping one hand on Dario's shoulder, Mo shepherded him toward the entrance to the apartments, wondering vaguely where Rosa had gone. Then he had to let go of Dario to run up the stairs, Dario's footsteps echoing his.

The apartment door was open. He could hear someone walking quickly. He stepped inside, and Rosa was coming toward him with clothes draped over her arm.

She smiled, and he wondered at the hint of sadness in her eyes. "Mo! I'm so happy for you. Congratulations. I'm taking all my stuff out. You'd better—" She stopped and gazed behind him at Dario, her mouth open, an *Oh shit!* look on her face.

He turned around and stepped back. "Dario, I'd like you to meet Rosa Fabrini, the sous-chef. Rosa, my son Dario."

"How wonderful to meet you." She dropped her clothes on a chair, stepped up to Dario. They shook hands, and she clasped his with both of hers, beaming into his face, looking up a couple inches.

She stepped back and scooped up her clothes. "I'm sure you two want to talk. I'll just put these in my closet." She nodded her chin at Dario. "I live in the other apartment. I had a...moth infestation, and my closets needed fumigating. Your father let me put my clothes in his extra room." She headed past them. "It should be fine to put my clothes up again. I'll get the rest of my stuff later. Thanks, Mo."

She closed the door behind her before he could say anything. Staring at the closed door, he felt a sinking inside him.

No. He wasn't letting her go. No damn way.

"Dad?" Dario asked.

Mo closed his eyes for a second then turned to his son. Later. He would talk to Rosa later. "This is the best day in my life. I'll get you something to eat and drink. When did you get here? How did you get here? How did you find me?"

His son was with him. No matter what else was going on in his life, he was happy for that.

And then it struck him.

"Your mom. Does she know?"

Dario's expression changed in a snap of a second. Open to closed. A smile to a scowl.

"I won't go back to her." Dario's face tightened and tendons stood out on his neck. "I think they know about you."

"Tell me." Mo heard his harsh tone but couldn't change it. This could be life or death for him.

"I found your restaurant on the computer before Christmas," Dario said in a rush of words. "After you left, I remembered that when I was a kid, you and I went fishing. You said when I grew up, we could start our own restaurant and call it Mo's Place. After you left, every once in a while, I'd look for the name. Then one day I saw it."

"You remembered all these years." Looking at the misery in Dario's face, Mo suspected Dario remembered it out of desperation.

What the hell had Theresa done to him?

Sure, she'd spent a lot of time with her friends, but she'd been a decent mother. A better parent than him, with all the hours he worked at the restaurant.

Dario nodded. "You didn't make fun of me."

"Someone's making fun of you?"

Dario shrugged and kind of sank into himself. Already different from the kid he'd hugged downstairs.

"Yeah."

"Who?"

"I'm smart," Dario said.

"I know. You've always been smart."

"The others, they don't understand. I'm not cool."

"Who are the others?"

"Tommy's kids." Dario crossed to the front window, his head down, his thin shoulders hunched.

"Tommy who?" Mo's hands curled into fists, and a name burned inside his gut. The only adult Tom he knew who still called himself Tommy.

"Tommy Di Luca."

He closed his eyes and clenched his teeth. His mind screamed *nooooo!*

"Dad?"

Taking a deep breath, he opened his eyes. "Why are you hanging around with Tommy's kids? Why would what they say matter to you?"

"I guess you don't know."

"Know what?"

"Mom married Tommy."

He shook his head. "Your mom said we couldn't divorce because we were married in the Catholic Church. She made me promise never to marry again. Maybe she's living with him and just saying—"

"Mom got a divorce from you four months after you left. Her lawyer's a friend of Tommy's."

He closed his eyes. Of course Tommy had a lawyer friend who specialized in divorce. With no one around to contest it, it must've been a slam-dunk.

"Are you okay, Dad?"

He nodded. He was the one who was supposed to worry about his son, not the other way around. "And Tommy knows about this place?"

Color surged into his face. "It's all my fault, but no one was supposed to touch my computer. I didn't know they'd see your website."

"It's not your fault." He forced himself to smile then to deepen and lower his voice so he sounded almost like himself. So Dario couldn't hear the anger and the dismay roiling inside him like a live, poisonous snake trying to twist out. "Don't worry. It will be okay. We'll have to leave and find another place."

"I'm going with you."

"Of course you are," he said.

The door opened, and he snapped around, standing in front of his son who was taller than him already. He stared straight at Rosa's face, the woman he loved who looked as pale as a zombie right now.

And it was all because of him.

27

"I was just coming to get the rest of my clothes and heard you talking." Rosa felt as if the world had spun the wrong way, and she was on the upside-down side.

From the misery on Mo's face, he felt the same thing.

She was aware of Dario's gaze shifting from her to him. Adding up the numbers, which wasn't hard since it was one man and one woman and one apartment.

But she couldn't worry about that now. Not when her life was falling apart again.

"You're leaving Miracle?" she asked.

"I'm sorry you had to hear."

"Sorry I had to hear?" She heard the sharpness in her voice and knew she was going to say and do the wrong things. Like yelling at Tony when he went into the deep end of Miracle Lake when he was only five and couldn't swim. Screaming because she'd been so scared. Everyone at the lake looking at her as if she were the worst mother in the village.

"I have to leave. I'm sorry for that, but I have no choice."

"Were you even going to tell me?"

"I was. I just found out."

"You—" She stopped. Put a hand to her stomach, because she hurt so bad. The anger slipping away, leaving just the hurt like a fire in her belly. Worse, in her heart. She backed up, her hand out as if to ward them off. But Mo and Dario weren't moving. Just staring at her as she made a fool out of herself.

"It's my fault," Dario said. "I did this."

"Did what?"

"Left my computer on, and now people can guess where my dad is."

"What people?"

Dario looked at Mo. "You didn't tell her?"

"I couldn't." He stared at her. "It could get you killed."

"You're a spy?" she asked.

He laughed, and she wanted to hurt him. Then she wondered how she could be angry right now at someone she...cared so much about. Someone who might go away and she might never see again.

"Think again. It's New Jersey. What's in New Jersey?"

"Jersey Shore? The ocean? Gardens?"

He and Dario looked at each other, the kind of look men sometimes did while talking to a woman and she didn't get it. The kind of look women exchanged when a man didn't get it.

"Remember the rumors going around about me being in the Mafia?"

"No." She shook her head. "Not you. That's something Linda Wegner made up just because you have a New Jersey accent."

"In that case, Linda Wegner will be one happy woman." He glanced at Dario. "The village gossip."

"You're kidding." Dario's eyes rounded. "There's really a village gossip? You told me about it in your letters, but I thought you were kidding."

"Forget the gossip." She slashed the air with her hand. "There's *always* gossip. It's like rain or snow. Something you can't stop. But the Mafia... You're joking, aren't you? There isn't really a Mafia anymore. That's just TV."

Mo shook his head. "Wish I could say you're right, but

it's as real as guns and bullets. There is a Mafia, and they're after me."

"I thought... I don't know. That they were broken."

"Like a lamp?" Mo said, and Dario laughed. But his laughter had a high note. A desperate note.

"It's not like the old days, is it?" she asked. "They don't have the same power."

"Didn't you watch the Sopranos?" Dario asked.

"We owned a restaurant, and I worked nights. I *still* work nights."

"The Mafia is alive and flourishing in Jersey," Mo said.

"All right, I can believe that." She had no choice. She knew Mo. He wasn't a man to run from an imagined trouble. "But you're not in New Jersey now. You're in Miracle, Wisconsin."

"It's not outer space. There's a highway out there." He gestured toward the front window. "Anyone can drive down it. They're probably making arrangements as I speak."

"They're probably on the way already." Dario sent a nervous look in the direction of the highway.

"With guns," Mo added.

"Guns?" She never thought guns were funny, but laughter, edged with hysteria, shrieked out of her throat. As she laughed, father and son stared at each other and she could read the silent this-woman-is-insane looks in their faces.

Her laughter changed, on the edge of turning into sobs. She sucked it in and stopped herself. They stared as she gasped out a breath then put her hand to her throat and swallowed. Only then could she talk.

"This village... Do you know what's around here?" She swept her arm out.

"Not much," Dario said. "A lot of fields covered with snow."

"Farms," Mo said. "The cheese factory."

"How about ducks, geese, rabbits, deer? This is hunting country. There's a weapon in nearly every home. More than one, I bet. Excluding children, probably four out of every five people in this town own rifles and shotguns."

"It's not the same." Mo shook his head. "They kill animals, not people."

"Not yet." She looked at Mo, holding his gaze, putting her will into it, everything she had because he was everything she needed. Everything she loved. "But we protect people. Especially our own."

"That's still not the same thing."

"It's not the same, it's better." She stood with her legs braced, with her head up, her voice urgent, her tone passionate. She had to make him believe what she was saying. "We're more determined than any Mafia guy because we *care*. Caring is powerful. Remember how the whole town got together to help Trish and Gunner when they were broke and expecting quads?"

"Quads? You mean babies?" Dario blinked.

"Yes, babies. And they already had two boys." She shifted her gaze to Mo; he was the one she needed to convince. "Remember Earl Raasch's video? When he said everyone in Miracle was his family. Well, you're living here now. You're part of the Miracle village and part of our family, like it or not."

Mo nodded, but his somber gaze remained on her. "Gunner and Trish lived here most of their lives. They were born here."

"It doesn't matter. You've lived here long enough to get accepted. You're the one that opened up your place to tape the videos for Gunner and Trish. Mo's Place is a favorite gathering place. You're part of our everyday lives." Rosa felt Dario's stare, but she kept her gaze on Mo, this stubborn, bullheaded *man*. "You think you can do everything yourself, but you aren't by yourself. There are people who care for you." She put her hands on her hips. "I'm not letting you go."

"How are you going to stop me?"

"By telling you the truth. Are you letting a bunch of bullies push you around?"

"They're not kids on a playground."

"I don't care how big they are. They're still bullies. And you know what you're acting like, don't you?"

"Holy shit," Dario said in a half whisper.

Mo looked at her blankly. Not answering. His brows lowered.

"A coward," she continued, "that's what. You ran once. Are you going to let your son see you run away again?"

"You don't get it."

"Dad's right," Dario said. "Anyone in our part of Jersey can tell you what they're like."

She slanted her gaze to him. "Does this look like Jersey to you?"

He shook his head.

Her gaze flicked back to Mo. "Does it look like Jersey to you?" she demanded, her voice sharp as a chef's knife, her heartbeat speeding. She wanted him to stay, but more important, she wanted him to live.

He didn't take his eyes off her. "What do you propose to do?"

"First of all, call Jerry."

Mo turned to Dario. "The village constable."

"Cool."

"No, it's not cool. There's not even a jail in the village."

"He's a very good shot," Rosa said. "And it's not like they'll send a gang of men over here, right?"

"One or two," Mo said. "Probably one."

"That's it?" She raised her eyebrows. "Are you afraid of one man?"

"One hitman? Yes, I am." He looked sideways at Dario. "I'll have to send you back."

Dario's mouth turned sullen. "I won't go."

Mo sighed. "I didn't think so." He turned back to Rosa. "Jerry's only one man. He'll need backup."

"You'll have backup." As she spoke, she couldn't believe what she was proposing. It was still hard to believe that it was happening. That the Mafia was coming to her little village. And she was planning to rally the whole community to fight it?

It was insane.

She wondered if Katie had a pie for that and had to stop an urge to laugh hysterically. "I can promise you—"

A hard knock on the door stopped her. She started. Mo turned to Dario and, in a harsh voice, said, "Go to the bedroom."

Dario looked at his father, his chin out, and said, "No."

The knock came again.

Mo put his hands to each side of his head. "This day's going to hell."

28

"The door from the break room was unlocked, so I thought I'd come up instead of calling you." Scotty stood inside Mo's living room, and he looked like a different man than Mo saw five days a week: his expression serious, his back straight, and his shoulders squared. "I heard you. Whatever happens, I'm in."

Mo believed him. Scotty was the kind of insane person who would do something like this. He lived by his instincts, which was probably why his dating life was a disaster until his newest girlfriend. And Mo wasn't so sure about her, either, but he wasn't about to put down another person. Not after the way he'd screwed up his own life.

"I can tell everyone." Scotty's eyes narrowed. "I'll call my hunting buddies."

"Wait!" Mo had seen some of Scotty's hunting buddies hanging around his bar. Not guys he'd want to put against a Mafia enforcer unless it was a beer-drinking contest.

"Before we do anything," Rosa said, "we should call Jerry."

"Not until you hear me out," Mo said.

Both Rosa and Scotty pressed their lips together. He could tell Rosa was quivering with impatience while Scotty frowned.

"I ran a restaurant in Jersey. It was my dad's, and I inherited it. The Di Luca Family would go there when my dad owned it. I knew a lot of them from the neighborhood. My Uncle Pete was in the Family—"

"A lieutenant," Dario said, a note of pride in his voice.

Somewhere inside Mo, he wept. "That's not a good thing to be."

Dario looked down at his lap. "I know. Especially after what happened to Uncle Carl."

"My cousin," Mo said to Rosa and Scotty. "Pete's son. He was found dead in a dumpster. A bullet hole in his forehead."

"We heard he skimmed money," Dario said.

"Carl and I grew up in the same building, and we were best friends. Everyone around us had big families except us." Mo stopped talking and swallowed. This next part wasn't going to be easy. "Then we grew up. I was working. Carl was... Well, one day about three years ago, he asked me for a loan, and I told him no."

"Was something wrong with him?" Rosa asked.

"He was a gambler," Dario said.

"A bad one. The *goomba*. He collected from the bookies. He knew gambling was a losing game. A game for suckers." Anger shook Mo, tangling with loss. "When he was whacked, I knew he must've been skimming," he continued though his voice was choked. "I was angry at everyone. Myself included."

"I was angry, too," Dario said, his eyebrows slanting down. "I liked Uncle Carl."

Grief washed over Mo, heating his face and prickling his eyes. He swallowed again before going on, his voice thick with emotion. "Every time the family came to eat at my restaurant, they sat at the same tables. Everyone knew about it. So when the FBI asked me to plant bugs at the tables, I said yes." He turned to Dario. "I had to do it for Carl."

Dario nodded but looked like he wanted to cry.

"And they found out?"

"After the third arrest of one of their guys, they figured it out."

"So you left New Jersey?" Rosa asked. "You left your family?"

"He didn't want to!" Dario stepped closer to him. "He wanted us to go with him, and my mom said no."

Scotty and Rosa stared at Mo with identical expressions of sympathy. Mo waved his hand, as if erasing their pity. "The Feds wanted me to go into WITSAC. They wanted to choose my new profession, and I didn't want that. I left the management of my restaurant to my wife until Dario was old enough to take it over." He had to reach up to rub Dario's hair. "I took some money and signed all my investments over to her and Dario, talked to my lawyer, then left."

When he'd left their Jersey home, Dario had been a head shorter than him. Now he was a couple inches taller.

Another hurt added to the pile of hurts.

"I ended up here," he said. "I didn't think they'd ever find me."

"It's my fault. Leaving your website up on the computer. Without that, stupid Tommy would never have found out."

"It's not your fault. I should've used a different name for the restaurant."

"But that was *our* restaurant name." Dario's face contorted. "Something you just told me. Mom didn't even know. It was *our* dream."

Seeing the misery in his face broke Mo. A guttural sound came from his throat, and he hugged Dario, who hugged him back tightly, his fingers digging into the back of Mo's shoulders.

When they drew apart, both of them were blinking

and sniffing, their breaths harsh.

"So this Tommy told the family?" Scotty asked.

"He had to," Dario said.

"He's their lawyer."

"Well, shit," Scotty said.

"And my stepdad."

"Double shit."

"No, he's a triple shit."

"A shithead," Scotty agreed, and Rosa poked his arm with her elbow. He yelped and rubbed his arm. "So what are we going to do now?"

Mo checked his watch. "The restaurant's open in five minutes, and you have hungry people to feed."

"I can't cook," Scotty said. "I've gotta protect you."

"No." Mo shook his head hard then turned to Dario. "When did this happen? When did Tommy see the computer? When did you leave?"

"Last night. I caught him in my room, looking at your website on my computer, and I yelled at him. He yelled back, then Mom came up, and we all had a big fight. I told Mom if anything happened to you, I'd never forgive her. That I'd leave and never talk to her again. And she just yelled at me that..." He closed his mouth, his jaw trembling. "It doesn't matter. But she told Tommy not to do anything until she thought about it. I stayed awake all night and, after two this morning, I heard Tommy tiptoe to his office."

He stopped to breathe noisily, sounding like one of the kittens just before it threw up. His face was tense and red, as if tears were close behind. "I knew he was calling behind Mom's back. I snuck out and got lucky. There was a cab cruising down the street. I flagged it, and when I got to the airport, I got lucky again and caught a plane right away that took me straight to Milwaukee. It almost felt like someone was..." He shook his head and looked at Mo. "Never mind. At least mom must've told him not to tell on you, or he wouldn't've been calling while she was asleep."

A knot in Mo's belly twisted. He wanted Dario to be right about Theresa but wasn't sure. Theresa was a proud woman. Proud of herself. Proud of her heritage. Proud of her place in the church.

Losing face because of him probably hadn't been easy.

Losing money... That would've been harder. He knew the restaurant wouldn't do as well without him. He'd been the heart of the restaurant. She never worked there and would have to hire someone to manage it. And when he told her he was keeping it in his name until Dario was old enough to take it over, she'd been furious, hate burning in her eyes.

Then there was the religion. If he were dead, the first thing she would do was start making plans for another ceremony with Tommy, this time in the church. She'd do it with a clear conscience, not feeling any guilt for her complicity in it.

After all, she wouldn't have pulled the trigger. And wasn't it Mo's fault for letting the Feds bug his place?

The night he'd left, she'd screamed at him. Saying he cared more for his cousin than her.

And to marry Tommy so soon... She must have been having an affair with him while they were married.

"They wouldn't send someone immediately," he said, stopping his useless thoughts. "We probably have at least a day's grace." He nodded at Scotty. "I'll go downstairs."

"While you're working, I'll call Jerry," Rosa said.

"Wait until I can talk to him, too."

"This is your life at stake." Her eyes flashed as if she were a warrior woman. "I'm not waiting for anything."

He stared at her, and his love for her whirled up inside him. So strong he couldn't speak. He had to brace his legs to keep from going to her and—

A small sound brought his attention to his side. Dario was looking at him with pity. Then Dario's gaze shifted to Rosa, with the same pity in his eyes.

He knew. Mo raked his fingers through his hair. Of course Dario knew. Just as Scotty and Lisa knew. Dario probably knew the second they walked into his apartment and he saw Rosa taking her clothes out, telling Dario the lame excuse. Dario wasn't stupid. The only stupid one in this situation was himself.

He stepped over to her. Put his arms around her back, held her tightly against him.

Her arms folded around his back, holding him just as tightly.

Then he released her. "I have to go downstairs now. Don't call Jerry until later." He turned to Dario. "And you stay here."

He left before either of them could argue with him, Scotty tagging after him.

And he knew as he ran down the stairs that Rosa was picking up the phone to tell Jerry the Mafia was coming to the village of Miracle.

29

The first thing Rosa did was call Jerry and tell him to come to Mo's.

The second thing was to tell Mo's fretting son that there were kittens in the other apartment and they needed to bring them into his dad's apartment. Though Dario was seventeen, his eyes brightened. After all this talk about Mafia and rifles, kittens were a nice change.

Rosa guessed his mother's choices were bothering him, too.

Just like her choice had made Nick turn on her.

"I don't like to leave them alone," she said, her voice thicker than usual as she led the way to the other apartment. "They need to get used to humans."

She opened the door to see the kittens wrestling. They stopped with their front legs wrapped around each other and stared at Dario and her. Rosa crouched and talked softly to them, and they untangled and padded to her. She grabbed Checkers first, having already identified him as the naughty one, and told Dario to put Pie into the carrier.

"You're just taking them down the hall," Dario said, obeying her despite Pie's squawks. "Why don't you let them follow us?"

"You've never had cats, have you?"

Dario stood. "My mom doesn't like dogs or cats."

"Some people don't." She took his place in front of the carrier gate. She opened it just far enough to slide Checkers in, then she quickly closed the gate. "Dogs follow people without questions. Cats only follow when they want to follow."

"Then I guess I like dogs better. This is a dump."

The knees on her slacks were dusty, and she swiped at them. "Your dad is going to fix it up."

"You've been staying at his place, haven't you?"

She stopped brushing the dust off her knees and looked him in the eyes. "Yes."

"I'm glad you didn't lie."

"Your dad told me you were smart. Will you carry the litter box?"

He laughed, looking surprised, and she shrugged. Mike used to say she was a pragmatist, and she supposed he was right. But pragmatists didn't have meltdowns and tantrums. After she first found out about Mike and Amber, she'd erupted like Mount Vesuvius.

Now she realized it was the best thing that had happened to her since she'd had her children.

And Mo. He was on the top of her *Best* list.

She should send a thank you note to Amber. She'd start it off with, *Thank you for being a whore.*

"I'll stay here," Dario said. "I can clean."

"Your dad won't let you." She lifted the carrier.

"You must know him well."

She strode past him to the hall, not answering. Sometimes the best thing to say was nothing.

In Mo's living room, she let the kittens out. They ran straight to the small second bedroom to their food and water, which she hadn't had time to transport before Mo and Dario came up.

"You have a weapon?" Dario asked.

"My most lethal weapons are words and brains." The doorbell rang, and she held up her hand. "Stay here while I get it."

"No, wait! We should call my dad. It might be the

hitman."

"Do Mafia hitmen normally ring the doorbell to announce themselves?"

He stared at her with his mouth open. While she ran downstairs, she gave herself a quick lecture. She had to watch her mouth in the future. Dario was young and wasn't used to her brand of sarcasm, while she was accustomed to treating young men like half idiots. Not all the time, but sometimes they needed it.

Other times she treated them as if they were precious. Especially Nick, her baby. He'd been more insecure than Matt and Tony who were close in age and were friends.

Thinking about Nick, a sadness kicked in. She breathed deeply and kicked it back out. She didn't have time for self-pity.

Dario's footsteps clumped on the steps behind her. He was protecting her. Just in case.

The thought warmed her. She liked this son of Mo's. Maybe Mo and his ex-wife had problems, but Dario seemed like a great kid.

In the hall, she waited for Dario before she opened the door. Not that she was afraid, but because young boys and young men and even older men needed to feel useful. Later, she might be more cautious, but logistically she couldn't imagine how the Mafia would get here this quickly. Only a kid would do something so impulsively and so fast. Throw clothes into a dufflebag, hail a cab, and just go. And then get lucky enough to catch a plane that was about to leave the airport right away and had an empty seat. Not only that, but a plane that didn't have any transfers.

She opened the door and wasn't surprised to see the village constable. "Hi, Jerry."

He nodded at her, but his gaze fell on Dario behind

her, checking him out as he entered. She and Dario backed up. In this small hallway, three was a crowd. Jerry stomped snow off the soles of his leather boots on the hall mat. The walkway was shoveled, but he must have stepped in a patch of snow on the way.

"What's so important?" he asked.

"It's complicated," she said. "Maybe we should talk upstairs."

He squinted curiously at Dario then her. "About Mike?"

"Please. I have a lawyer who plans to inflict damage on Mike." As he laughed, she turned to Dario and squared her shoulders. "You may as well know. I'm divorcing my husband."

Dario frowned.

"Not her fault," Jerry said. "He was cheating on her."

She introduced them quickly then headed upstairs so they'd have to follow. In the living area, she gestured for Jerry to sit on the sofa. Dario stood in front of the big window that overlooked Main Street, radiating uneasiness.

Sinking in the easy chair, she wished she could do something for him...then realized she was. She was working to keep his father safe.

"You ready to tell me what's so important?" Jerry asked.

"Are you ready to keep an open mind?"

"My middle name is Open Mind."

"Good. Then you won't blink when I tell you the Mafia is after Mo."

"Well, shit," he said.

She nodded. That sounded like an open mind to her. Instead of *well, shit,* he could've said *bullshit.*

In the conversation that followed, Dario's head went

back and forth as she and Jerry spoke quickly. He asked
if she'd been drinking; she suggested he was scared and
his brother who had PTSD might be a better person to
handle this. Instead of taking offense, he laughed and
sighed. Gazing at her with lovesick eyes, he asked if she
was ready to date younger men. She glanced at Dario
(who was listening with his jaw dropped) and told him
that when Jerry wasn't working his constable job, he was
a professional flirt.

She turned back to Jerry. "I might, but my dance card
is full."

"She's with my dad," Dario said.

Rosa closed her eyes. Dario was sweet, but she wished
he would keep his mouth shut.

"I know." Jerry put his hand over his chest. "My heart
is broken."

Rosa opened her eyes. Of course he knew already.
Scotty and Lisa had already let her know the bad news.
Besides, this was Miracle. The home of mosquitoes in
summer, snowmobilers in winter, and gossips year
round. She was surprised Mike hadn't called yet and
screamed at her for cheating, not realizing the irony.

But possibly he was out of the gossip loop. After all,
he wasn't the most popular person in Miracle. She'd only
found out after their break up that his nickname was The
Italian Tyrant.

"Jerry doesn't mean anything by his flirting," she said
to Dario. "He thinks he's funny and doesn't know he's
not."

"Are you taking lessons from my sister-in-law?" Jerry
grinned.

She shrugged. His sister-in-law, Nia, had a brain
injury that had wiped away all social skills along with her
memories before she woke up in a hospital with her head

bandaged. Her bluntness made some people uneasy, but Rosa found it a pleasure to talk to someone who told the truth. "Another time we can joke and flirt. This is serious."

"If the Mafia is coming, you should call the sheriff's office."

"Would they believe Mo? Assign someone to watch him?"

"Maybe. At the least, they'd take him in protective custody."

"My dad could've done that before," Dario said. "He wouldn't go then, and he's not going now."

"He'd have to." Jerry leaned an elbow on his chair arm, his shoulder hunching up. "They're not going to let him continue to run the restaurant under a fake name."

Dario's lower lip stuck out, and he headed toward the hall door. As he passed her, she leapt off the chair and grabbed the back of his sweatshirt.

"Stay," she ordered before turning to Jerry, who remained on the couch, a wary look on his face that said more than words that shit was coming to Miracle soon.

The look on his face was right.

But it was up to them to stop the shit before it happened.

"*That's* the help you plan on giving Mo?" She swung her arm out. "Throwing him to the law?"

"I'm the law."

"I babysat you." She put her hands on her hips. "I changed your diaper."

"That's not true."

"Ask your mom."

"I will." He'd had the same stubborn look when he was young. "I have to do something. I was elected to keep the law."

"Wrong again."

He rolled his eyes but was smart enough to keep his mouth shut.

"You were elected to serve the people in the village so we don't have to call the sheriff." She crossed her arms. "You're the man who's supposed to take care of us while keeping us out of trouble. That's the reason we have our own constable instead of a deputy poking his or her nose into our business."

"What happens in Miracle stays in Miracle?"

"Exactly." She lowered her arms and gave him The Stare. "You know that, Jerry. I can name a few instances in your own family when that code came in handy."

He rolled his eyes. "So you want me to fight the Mafia."

"Yes."

"Not alone," Dario said. "She wants the whole town to fight the Mafia."

Jerry looked at him and then at Rosa. "You know how crazy this sounds?"

"You're not John Wayne. You won't have to do it alone."

"I'm not asking Rob. Not with his PTSD."

"Rob isn't the only one in Miracle who knows how to use a weapon. Tony will join you. Scotty will. Sam Guthrie will. Even Earl Raasch will. I'm sure we easily have one hundred men and probably fifty women who can help you."

"You're crazy. I'm not asking the whole town to arm themselves to protect your lover."

She kept The Stare on him. Compelling him not to obey her but to believe what she said. "You don't have to ask anyone. I'll ask them and you can turn a blind eye. If there are any repercussions, I'll swear on a Bible that you didn't know anything about it."

Frowning, he looked down, breaking the stare first.

Inside, she exulted. But she still stood there, unmoving. Until the words were said, she would not relax. She would not let her guard down.

"Hunting season is just about over," he said. "The only legal game out there is just a few small animals no hunter wants to bother with. At least this would keep the idiots busy and out of the farmers' fields."

Her heart thumped, and she was aware of Dario's wide-eyed gaze on her. "I'll start calling people."

Jerry stood. "No. Before I do anything, I need to talk to Mo."

As he left to go downstairs, she held herself back from following. Mo needed to do this on his own. She would have to do something very hard. Stay here and wait.

30

Jerry stopped in the doorway, gazing back to give her a stern look. "*I'll* start calling people. *You* call Tony, and that's it." His voice was more commanding than she'd heard it before. "Make sure he doesn't tell anyone until I say it's okay. Especially his Tomahawk buddies. We don't want anyone outside of Miracle knowing about this."

She nodded. No one outside of Miracle would believe the Mafia was coming to Miracle. If she didn't live here, she wouldn't believe it.

He stomped out. She listened to him head to the staircase then thump down the stairs. Only when she heard the door close did she turn to Dario.

"We did it," she said, and her voice shook. "He's actually doing what I said."

"*You* did it." Awe shined in Dario's eyes, as if she were the Madonna come to life. "I was afraid my dad would get killed because of me. It would've been all my fault."

"Don't think that way. It wouldn't have been your fault. Of course you would look up your father. I would've done the same thing. Anyone would have."

"But I shouldn't have left the computer on with the website open."

"You didn't know your stepdad would sneak into your bedroom. Surely he has his own computer."

"I knew he was going on it. Looking at porn places, the perv. I knew and just—"

"Stop!" She gave him her dark frown along with The Stare. A double whammy of fierceness. "Your stepdad is the one at fault. Not you. You're nearly eighteen and you have a right to privacy. Isn't that so?"

"Yes, but—"

"No buts! The answer is yes, and it's all his fault."

Dario's face contorted. He started heaving and nodding and sucking in air. His face turned red, and moisture glittered in his eyes.

She stood, ready to shout for Mo and yell that his son was having an attack. Maybe asthma. Then it hit her that he was holding back tears. She stepped toward him, her arms lifting. Then footsteps pounded into the room.

Mo. His face tensed. His mouth twisted as if in pain.

She jumped back to let him grab Dario and hold him close while Dario clasped him back.

"I was afraid it was my fault," Dario said in between gasping sobs. "I was so afraid."

"It's not," Mo said.

His face bent against the side of Mo's head, Dario nodded and wheezed. "I know. Rosa told me, so I know it's true."

He started to sob steadily, and she headed past him to the bedroom with the kittens. But what she really wanted to do was cry with Dario.

She was shaking. So afraid she was doing the wrong thing, talking Mo into staying. He might die. A lot of men and women in Miracle might die. Including her middle son.

Then she'd be the one sobbing. It would all be her fault.

31

Mo was glad the lunch hour was slow, normal on a Wednesday, with only a half dozen tables filled plus a few stragglers at the bar, drinking beer and eating bar food or pasta with Rosa's meat sauce. He was running on automatic, greeting guests, chatting, and handing out drinks. Getting the sodas for Lisa. Even laughing and making jokes. Doing it all with a fraction of his brain while the other fractions were spinning ideas that they then knocked down. Like beer bottles off a shelf, one by one.

In these short seven months he'd lived here, he'd fallen in love with a woman. More than he'd ever loved a woman in his life. It felt to him that he'd been walking around in a gray fog before he met her, and now sunshine surrounded him. And then there was this village where people stuck together. The Di Lucas called themselves a Family, but *this* was what a real family did.

And Dario... With every letter he'd sent to Dario, he'd told Dario that a piece of his heart was missing.

Now that piece of his heart was back in place, sewn in with big sloppy stitches. And his whole heart was so full of love for everyone, he wanted to jump on the bar and sing "Hallelujah."

But because of him, trouble was on its way to this little Wisconsin village. And trouble that involved the Di Lucas often came with a friend: death.

Upstairs, Rosa with her passionate speech had convinced him he needed to stay. That leaving would be wrong. But now he was away from her, and his emotions had cooled enough for him to think instead of just feel. Rosa didn't know that the Mafia was like a many-headed snake. Shoot off one head, and before you could pull the trigger again, another head took its place.

Leo Di Luca wasn't going to let a dot on a map beat him. The Feds hadn't beaten Leo, not even after they'd bugged his restaurant. Just three arrests and only one conviction. One jerk not important enough to be a snake head.

The strongest and toughest union guys had caved in to the Di Lucas. For decades they'd been taking their vig from storekeepers. Politicians were stuffed in their back pockets, right next to their bulging wallets. And that wasn't counting the ties to gambling, prostitution, and drugs.

He would tough out this day. Tomorrow would be the earliest anyone would make it here. Might even be the following day.

Whoever it was would be making the trip for nothing.

By then he'd be gone.

His spirit dull, he watched Jerry march up to him, a grim look on his face.

Usually Jerry was a jokester, a good-time guy. With this stern face, he looked more like his twin, the former army sergeant and now artist who lived with his wife in the Witch's House on Miracle Lane. Jerry stopped at the side of the bar.

"I need to talk to you."

"I have to bartend," Mo said.

Jerry nodded at the three guys on barstools who'd stopped talking to watch them. "Either of you any good at pouring drinks?"

Howard Horshley, who sang at the Lutheran church every Sunday, raised his hand. "I have a bar at home."

"Want to take care of this one? Mo here will give you a free meal today."

"Sure. But I don't know how to use the cash register."

"Tell 'em drinks are free until Mo gets back. But they need to tip the bartender."

The guys laughed, but Mo didn't, and neither did Jerry, who was already heading to the back. Mo followed him past the kitchen and into the break room. It consisted of a long table with chairs. No ashtrays—anyone who wanted to smoke had better do so in the alley—but Mo thought the stale smell of cigarette smoke was imbedded in the walls.

He didn't take a chair, and neither did Jerry.

"I talked to Rosa," Jerry said.

Mo nodded, standing stiffly, trying to look relaxed. Trying not to show anything in his face. The stakes were too high to give anything away. Not just his happiness was at stake, but Dario's happiness and Rosa's happiness.

And not just his life was at stake, either. That was Dario's and Rosa's, too.

And if they did what Rosa wanted, the lives of every village resident would be at stake, all 634 of them.

"The Mafia stuff," Jerry said. "It sounds nuts."

"So do a lot of things that have gone on in Miracle lately. Some of that includes your twin."

"You got me there." Jerry scratched his jaw. "Why did you run? Why not go into witness protection?"

Mo didn't answer right away. The clock on the wall ticked, and music from the front filtered in. Reba McEntire and Kelly Clarkson singing "Because of You." He wasn't a country music fan but liked a variety of music, and he'd fallen in love with Reba's voice.

"You may as well tell me what you're thinking," Jerry

said.

"That I've always liked redheads."

Jerry didn't laugh. "You can stall me all day, I don't mind. But while we're shooting the shit here, old Horshley will be giving away drinks to everyone who comes in this place and raking in the tips."

"It's lunchtime. I doubt there will be a stampede. But thanks for that, anyway."

"Always glad to help. That's what we constables do. You ready to answer my questions?"

"The Feds said if I went into WITSEC, I wouldn't be able to work in a restaurant. They thought I should go into sales. Said I was good with people."

"You got Rosa, though I'm not seeing your charms."

"You're the wrong sex."

Jerry's mouth curved up into an almost smile. "The second reason?"

"I was never supposed to contact Dario. Ever. Not in my whole life."

"It was to protect him. And you."

"That's what they said."

"You didn't listen. And now Dario's here."

Mo closed his eyes tight. "Yes," he whispered, agony burning inside him. "Yes, he's here."

"And according to Rosa, the Mafia is coming."

He opened his eyes and saw Jerry's mouth twist with disbelief. "It's true."

"That's what she said. I don't want to believe it but—"

"Believe this, I wish it weren't true a thousand times more than you do."

"I'm not so sure about that. Rosa wants to involve the whole village. She insists that I don't call the sheriff's. You know what I've got to do?"

He nodded. "I understand. Just give me and my son a

few minutes to pack and clear out before the deputies come. I'd appreciate it."

"Wrong answer. She reminded me that I work for the citizens of Miracle, not the fuckin' Sheriff's Department."

"You're kidding." The darkness inside Mo lightened. He gave a crack of laughter.

"Wish I were kidding. It's going to be messy." Jerry's eyebrows slashed together. "Maybe deadly."

"It would be better if I just packed up and left."

"You should've thought of that before you started sleeping with Rosa."

Mo stared at Jerry. Not answering. But inside he howled like a sick dog.

"Ah, shit, forget I said that." Jerry scratched his jaw again. "What's done is done. Now we've got to make the best of it. Rosa wants me to call all the men with rifles and shotguns, but I talked her out of it. Just what you don't need in your bar."

"Drinking and weapons aren't a good mix."

Jerry shoved his hands in his pockets. "You know the Family better than I do." He frowned. "Is that what they call themselves? The Family?"

"No special names. Mob or Mafia, too, but Family is probably the most common."

"No kidding." Jerry's eyebrows rose. Though he'd been fairly cop-like up to now, Mo caught the aliveness on his face. The excitement. "So, you think someone'll show up?"

"I *know* someone will be here."

"Tonight?"

"Doubt it. But soon. They probably know Dario's here or is on his way." Pride rose up inside him for his son's resourcefulness. Dario had known what he needed to do, and he'd done it. And it had all gone so smoothly instead of the usual travel nightmare for anyone who didn't have a private plane. If he'd lived in Miracle, Linda Wegner would be telling everyone it was part of the miracle that had been prophesied last spring.

Frown lines creased Jerry's forehead, his eyebrows lowered. "What if the mob boss from Jersey calls his counterpart in Chicago and asks him to send one of their guys? That's only about five hours from here. They might be here any minute."

Mo shook his head. "They won't want the other Families to know I was loose in Wisconsin, running a restaurant. That my teenage son could find me and they couldn't. They wouldn't want to lose face over me. I'm not important enough."

"You sure? You might be underestimating your importance."

"*That* I'm positive about."

"So what would they do next?"

"I'd say they'll pick someone to do the hit." As he said the words so casually, his voice almost flat, disinterested, nothing seemed real. But he knew they were as real as the beer he'd been serving. As real as the floor he stood on. As real as his love for Rosa.

"He'll have to pack carefully," Jerry said. "You can't get an assassin's rifle though airport security in a carryon."

"I'm not an expert on Mafia hitmen." Mo frowned. "I fed them. I didn't arm them. But he'll probably rent a room at a motel or hotel nearby. Probably the nearest big city."

"Tomahawk, Wausau, or Eagleton?"

"One of them. I think whoever it is won't make it tonight. The logistics won't work. Tomorrow, though..."

Jerry's jaw set. "You're sure?"

"Ninety-eight percent."

"So, that's two percent uncertain."

"Life is always two percent uncertain." Mo rubbed the bridge of his nose and wondered what the percentages were that he'd make it through the week.

Jerry flipped out his cell phone. "The difference is that we don't always *know* it's two percent." He pressed a button then put the phone to his ear. He held up his hand with his index finger up, letting him know he'd be a minute. "Hey, Sarah," he said, his head down, "I have to be on the job tonight. I'll be busy tomorrow, too. Maybe the next day."

He listened, nodded, said goodbye, and closed his cell phone. "Looks like I'm sleeping over tonight," he said.

Jerry's expression was grim, as if he didn't have much hope. Mo felt the same hopelessness yawning inside of him. Right now it seemed impossible to him that anything good would come of this.

32

Rosa rolled out of the narrow bed in the guest room alone. She grabbed a sweater to wear over her nightgown because her robe was still at the house Mike had taken over.

By now she thought even Mike had heard about her and Mo. By now he was probably kicking himself because what he'd done had forced them together.

Despite her worries about the day ahead, the thought cheered her, and she didn't feel guilty. There was nothing wrong with embracing scraps of joy.

Crossing the room, she remembered to avoid the litter box. After using the bathroom, she saw that Jerry was conked out on the couch with Checkers purring on the couch arm next to his head. Stretched out with his mouth open and light streaking from the blinds across his forehead, Jerry looked younger than thirty. As if his troubles had lifted during his sleep. She hoped so, because she was afraid of what the day would bring. Very afraid.

From Mo's bedroom came the sound of snoring, either Mo or Dario.

Noises came from the kitchen. She peeked in and saw Tony. He'd come over last night, bringing with him two shotguns, four rifles, and boxes of ammunition. Reminding her how much he'd loved watching the old westerns on TV when he was a kid, with the showdowns between the good guys and bad guys, the dusty streets empty and the townsfolk hiding in their houses, only a few brave enough to peek out their windows.

He'd always wondered why someone didn't just grab a gun and shoot the bad guy. This scenario was his childhood fantasy come true.

Not Jerry's. When he'd seen the weapons, his mouth had thinned.

There was even a weapon for Rosa, but she preferred her chef's knife. She'd helped butcher a pig when she was young and lived with her parents. Though it was something she never wanted to do again, she would have no problem slicing through the thinner human skin.

A meowing, furred kitten weaved between her ankles. Rosa whispered to Pie that she'd feed her in a couple minutes, then she hurried into her room to change.

An hour later, the kittens had been fed with kitty food and the humans with omelets and toast and oranges, coffee was perked, and they'd all taken showers. As if they'd received a notice to be clean in case they would die today.

It was a workday, so Jerry's calls were limited. But by mid morning, there were four men with shotguns in the bike/motorcycle shop across the street, and in the knitting/sewing/crafting shop, Diane Freeman and her daughter, Michelle, both had their rifles loaded and had said they didn't need any damn men to help them.

Rosa admired them for that.

In Earl's Taxidermy and Reupholstery, both Earl and Gunner were armed. When Mo heard, he'd headed over there and ordered Gunner to go home. He had six kids and his wife depending on him.

Rosa could've told him it was a nice idea but useless. That the men in Miracle had spines like steel rods, and the women had spines like rubber, because rubber was flexible. And didn't women have to be flexible to do all things?

But some facts of life everyone had to learn for themselves.

On the other side was the volunteer firehouse. In the morning, there were only two men and two women. By midafternoon, there were a half dozen. After four p.m., when the cheese factory closed for the day, she lost count of the watchers in the downtown buildings and a few hardier hunters in vans and pickups and cars—waiting and watching.

At four thirty-four p.m., a car stopped across the street.

Jerry peered out the front window of Mo's apartment, the lowering sun slanted so no one could see in. "This is it," he said.

In the kitchen, Dario started to cross to him, and Mo grabbed the back of his shirt and pulled him back.

"How do you know?" Dario shook out of Mo's grip but stayed by him.

"I don't recognize the vehicle."

"You know every vehicle in this place?"

Moving back from the sofa, keeping low, Jerry said, "I know every vehicle, every person, every cat, and every dog."

"And if it's someone from Jersey," Mo said, crossing to the couch, "I'll know him."

Tony backed off the couch to make room for Mo. He and Jerry grabbed their jackets draped on the chair near the door. Mo peered out the window, and his shoulders stiffened. "Shit."

Dario jumped on the couch beside him and stared out the window. "Shit."

"You know him?" Jerry asked. "Looks young."

"He's my friend." Dario's voice rose.

Sitting on the easy chair, Rosa put Pie on the floor

and ignored the kitten's mew. She wanted to go over to the couch, but they'd all warned her to stay back. As if she were an easily wilted flower. She didn't like it, but since she wasn't holding a rifle or shotgun, she stayed where she was.

"He lived two blocks from us." Mo's face looked tortured, his eyes shadowed. "Bobby Franco. He's Leo Di Luca's nephew. A couple years older than Dario. When he was growing up, all the birthday parties were at my restaurant. He loved our polenta pudding. Damn it."

"What's he doing here?" Dario slammed his fist on the sofa back. "What the fuck is he doing here?"

Mo put his hand on his shoulder. Rosa crossed her arms to keep herself from walking over to him and hugging him. He had his dad and didn't need her.

At the doorway, Jerry called, "Mo and Dario, stay here. You, too, Rosa. I mean that."

Then he and Tony were in the hall, the door closed behind them.

Mo and Dario turned their heads and stared at the closed door. On both their faces, Rosa saw the longing to go after Jerry and Tony. Saw the agony because they couldn't. Dario because his dad wouldn't let him. Mo because he had to stay or Dario would go.

Rosa didn't have to be a mind reader to see that. She had the same agony. Her son would be on the street.

She crossed to the couch and knelt next to Mo.

All she could do now was wait and watch.

It was like the worst TV show in the world, but Mo couldn't stop watching. Tall and skinny Bobby with bad hair that all the grease in his restaurant couldn't tame was on the other side of the two-lane highway that was definitely not well traveled, strutting like a model on a highway. Such a Jersey snob that he didn't attempt to blend in. Too young and arrogant to think that anyone from the sticks would nail him.

"What a *goomba*," Dario said, and his voice wobbled.

"*Bastardo*," Rosa said with a perfect Sicilian accent that reminded Mo of his grandma on his mom's side.

On the sidewalk, Bobby's strut slowed. Mo grabbed the binoculars Jerry had left and put them to his eyes. Bobby's face was blurry, and he adjusted the lens in time to see Bobby's staring eyes and his mouth open with shock. Could practically see the *oh fuck* lighting up his tiny brain.

A car door closed.

Mo shifted the binoculars. Saw someone with his back to him step out of an SUV. One of the Schillings, he thought, and immediately forgave them for all the bad singing he'd suffered through. He vowed silently that when this was over, if he and Dario were still alive, he would prepare a feast for the whole damn village.

Another car door slammed.

And another.

Mo aimed the binoculars on Bobby again. His eyes were darting, his neck down like a turtle, trying to make himself a smaller target. He must've grown about six inches in the three years since Mo had fled Jersey, but he still had a couple pimples. It hurt Mo to look at him.

What the hell was his uncle doing, turning his immature nephew into a killer?

That's the only reason Bobby would be here: to whack Mo. To prove himself to the Don.

Bobby's mother, Gina, was friends with Theresa, Mo's ex. At least, as much as anyone could be friends with Gina, who had the personality of a rabid dog. Bobby's dad had moved to Florida when he was a kid, and Gina had raised him on her own. Mo wondered if she knew where Bobby was and what he was up to.

He had a crazy urge to call her and ask, *Do you know where your son is right now?*

"He's backing up," Dario said.

"Jerry's crossing the street." Rosa's voice was tense. "So is Tony."

Mo didn't take his gaze off Bobby. He wished to hell he was down there with the two men. If he could just talk to Bobby. Remind him of the—

Bobby's hand slid into his pocket, and every muscle in Mo's body tensed.

Dario's breath sucked in, and Rosa emitted a strangled moan. She grabbed Mo's arm above his wrist and squeezed so hard it hurt.

More car doors slammed. From the building behind Bobby, Mo saw two people exit, but still he kept his gaze on Bobby, sending him a silent message: *Don't shoot, don't shoot, don't shoot. Don't be an asshole.*

"Everyone's out there." Dario's voice rose with excitement. "Bobby won't get away."

Rosa's grip on Mo's arm didn't loosen.

"There must be about fifty rifles pointing at him," Dario said, and along with the excitement, Mo heard a sob. "He's toast."

Bobby's eyes darted from side to side, and when another door slammed behind him, he jumped and turned around. Like an animal being surrounded by a pack of wolves.

He did the only thing he could. What hunted animals did everywhere. He snapped around and ran toward the weakest link. Earl Raasch, the oldest villager on the street. His arm out, Bobby knocked down Earl then kept running. A couple dozen men chased after him.

"*Bastardo!*" Rosa shouted. "Get him. Get him. Get him."

"Jesus," Dario said.

Sick to his stomach, Mo aimed the binoculars at Earl and saw he'd fallen on a patch of snow. A couple men had stayed behind and were bending over him.

Mo put down the binoculars, thinking of the reason behind this whole thing. His cousin Carl who'd been a made guy and ended up dead before his time because he'd put his hand in the wrong till.

The running guys disappeared from their sight, and Dario jumped off the couch and dashed to the side window to keep track of them.

Mo turned to Rosa. She was staring across the street at Earl, her face pale. He knew she was worried about him. And probably thinking it could've been Tony who'd been knocked down. Or worse, Tony dead.

He put his arm around her back, and she turned to him. "That man...Dario's friend..." Her voice was a harsh whisper. "He would've killed you."

It took a couple seconds for his brain to get that she worried about what might have happened to *him*. His control broke. He made a sound like a half cry and drew her to him. Holding her as if he would never let her go.

"They got him!" Dario cried. "He's down!"

Rosa shuddered in Mo's arm and pushed away. As Dario whooped, she asked, "It's not over yet, is it?"

He looked into her beautiful, worried eyes and wished he could say it was all over.

But he shook his head. "No, it's not over."

33

"You can't do this," Bobby said, not looking dapper or cool anymore, tied to a chair and trussed up tighter than a UPS package.

Half the village gathered in the Village Hall, one of the most depressing and cold places Mo had been in. Yet he was far from depressed. So much emotion filled him he could pick only one that was uppermost.

Love.

For Dario.

For Rosa.

For Jerry.

For Tony.

For everyone in this tiny village where miracles happened. He felt an overwhelming surge of gratitude for every man and woman who'd given up their plans to be here for him. Some of them losing work time and pay he knew they needed. All of them doing it to protect him.

To illegally protect him.

To illegally form their own sentence for Bobby's crime.

As the target, Mo had a front row seat on the metal folding chair. The only one who had taken her coat off was Gloria, the real estate agent who was also on the village board. Thanks to Linda Wegner, everyone in the village knew she was having hot flashes.

Today Mo even loved the village's uncrowned gossip queen.

Gloria was speaking now. She sat between trussed-up Bobby and Earl who had a bandage on his forehead and a hang 'em high scowl, his jowls settled into grim folds.

"We have to be reasonable," Gloria said. "If we kill him and someone finds out, we might get sued. That's murder. Murder isn't legal, and our insurance doesn't cover illegal acts."

"It's not murder," a man shouted. "It's justice."

"I know a place to put his body," a reedy woman's voice called out, and Mo was pretty sure it was white-haired Agatha Schwitzer who'd celebrated her eightieth birthday at his place last month and got giddy on two glasses of red wine. "No one will ever find it."

More voices joined the two in agreement. Mo hadn't realized there were so many places in the area to dump a dead body.

"I almost feel sorry for Bobby," Dario said in a shaken voice, low enough for only Mo to hear.

Dario's hands were curled into fists on his thighs, and Mo squeezed the one nearest to him. Sweet Jesus, this was nuts.

"Stop it!" Earl's rough voice roared out. "We don't want to turn into animals like them, do we?"

The shouts subsided, but grumbles still came along with laughter that Mo suspected was gallows humor.

"We're not in an old western movie where people took the law into their own hands," Earl continued.

"Then what the hell are we doing here?" a Schilling asked, a bleat in his voice.

"Yeah!" a woman called. "And why is he wrapped like a side of beef ready to be put on a hook? We should just kill him and not waste any more time. If none of you got the balls to do it, I do."

With that last remark, Mo recognized a regular who was about fifty pounds overweight, drove a Harley, and was one of the best Karaoke singers in his place. If she'd sung the words instead of yelled them, he would've recognized her immediately.

"Mo tells me that this fellow…" Earl gestured at Bobby and there was a pause while everyone got a good look at the trussed-up skinny guy wearing his fur-collared leather jacket, his sallow complexion turned pasty, like curdled milk, and his eyes bugging out like a beagle's as he gawked at this crowd of rifle-carrying yokels.

A few derisive comments were called out. The kindest thing being said was that he looked like a spider with the extra legs cut off, wearing a squirrel on his head.

Mo didn't need to be psychic to guess Bobby was mentally kicking himself, wishing he hadn't underestimated the villagers. Wishing he'd spent more time planning the hit than he'd spent planning what to wear.

"This fellow," Earl began again, "is the nephew of the Mafia's leader, the guy they call the Don. I think we got a bargaining chip here." He stabbed his thumb in Bobby's direction. "Would you let anyone kill off your nephew?"

A few "hell yeah!" shouts came from the villagers, along with laughter that drowned out most of the protests.

"Maybe some of us would. But it's the board's opinion that we should call the Don and let him know that if he agrees to leave Mo alone, we'll take his word as a man of honor and send this young man home. What'll you all say?"

Dissent broke out. Questions about whether a man who dealt with prostitution and drugs and murder and other nasty things could be a man of honor. Until finally Earl said that there might be merit in what they said, and he stabbed a bent and wrinkled index finger toward Mo.

"You know the guy. What do you think?"

Mo looked at his son, whose agonized face reflected his own churning emotions. He turned back to the long table with the board members. "It can go either way. The Don has a lot of pride."

"Bobby's not his blood nephew," Dario said. "Bobby's his nephew from his wife's sister."

"That makes a difference?" Earl shook his head, his furry eyebrows contracting. "I don't think much of these mob guys."

"Even if he was blood," Mo said, "he wouldn't be the first Don to let a relative who screwed up take a hit."

"I know what we should do." Rosa stood; her commanding voice rang out. "We don't call the Don. We call his mother." She pointed at Bobby. "She'll call her sister, the Don's wife, and the wife will make sure the Don listens to our proposition."

Voices erupted. Mo fought a need to get to his feet, take Rosa in his arms, and kiss her breathless.

She was glorious! And she was his woman.

He didn't know how she felt, and he wasn't free to ask—not when he might be killed any day—but he loved her. Loved everything about her. Her pride, her intelligence, her loyalty, her cooking...

He'd fallen in lust with her looks, and then he'd fallen in love with the woman.

The urge to kiss her under control, he paid attention to what people were saying. Mostly women, agreeing with Rosa's take.

On the board table, Becky Niemow, who had the new-wife glow along with a nice-sized baby bump, leaned forward. "That's brilliant, Rosa. I give it my vote. And I think that since you're Italian—and a mom—you should be the one to call this fellow's mother."

A groan came from Bobby.

"How're we gonna get all their phone numbers?" someone asked.

"If he's got any brains," Earl jabbed a finger at Bobby, "he'll tell us right fast."

"If he had any brains," someone else called, "he'd be in college learning how to do something that doesn't include murder and prostitution."

"If he had brains," a new voice shouted, "he wouldn't've paraded down Main Street looking like he came straight from the Jersey Shore."

"It's all the hair spray he uses," another voice said. "I heard that hair spray destroys brain cells."

All the voices were familiar to Mo, but emotion was muffling them. They were all here for *him*. Doing this to save his sorry life.

He stood. Not saying anything. Just stood. Slowly the voices died, but he waited to speak until he could feel Linda Wegner mentally pushing him to say something that she could repeat over and over again.

"You're all assuming this will work. But as the one who caused all this, I've got to tell you it might explode in our faces. If one of you were killed..." He looked at all five board members, then turned to peer around the room, noticing for the first time that it was so crowded people were standing in the back. Whole families were here, not just parents. He even saw Nick, Rosa's youngest, at the end of the hall.

Emotion welled up again, closing his throat. He swallowed. Before it went any further, things needed to be said. He owed it to them. "One possible outcome is that the Don might hire pros to take care of this. He might send them here to take out the town. Leo Di Luca has a lot of pride, and I can't guess which way he'll go."

With his heart heavy, he sat down.

There were too many possibilities. Too many hidden traps. But dealing with a man who prided himself on his honor but in reality had no honor was not something that gave Mo a lot of faith.

If not for Dario, he would pack up what he needed, sign the bar over to Rosa, and drive away. Just like that.

But Dario had come here for him, and he couldn't—he *wouldn't*—take Dario with him to live as a fugitive for the rest of his life.

Especially since he knew Dario wouldn't leave him now. At seventeen, you had optimism. At forty, you had pragmatism. At seventeen, you had passion. So much passion that if someone lit a match, it could cause an explosion.

At thirty-eight, you still had passion, but you picked your battles.

And sometimes you left it in the hands of the villagers.

34

Rosa sat in the Village Hall office with Bobby's cell phone in her hand. She had an audience: Mo, Dario, Earl, Gloria, Jerry, and the sullen guest of honor, Bobby. Right now he was darting poisonous looks at Rosa that should've knocked her off the orange plastic chair that the village had bought in the 1950s and was now back in style. She should've been lying on the floor, pale and barely breathing, like an older—*much* older—Sleeping Beauty.

"You ready for this?" Earl asked.

She wished she had a glass of her favorite wine. Two glasses would be better. But all she had was water in a plastic cup, and she nodded, reminding herself that she was going to talk to a twenty-year-old boy's mother. That it didn't matter whether she lived in New Jersey or Wisconsin. She knew the pain the mother would feel. And if she were Bobby's mother, the only thing that would matter to her was that her son be safe. And to keep him safe, she would do anything and everything.

With a nod, she clicked on the phone number on his cell phone that simply said "Mom." As it rang, she pressed the speakerphone button.

A woman answered on the second ring. "Bobby! Why the hell didn't you call me sooner? I've been worried sick. Leo should never've given you that job. You'd better believe I told him so, too."

"Mrs. Pierno," Rosa said. "I'm calling on your son's phone about him."

Seconds of silence ticked by. Bobby opened his

mouth, and Jerry gripped his arm, reminding him that anything he said would make it worse.

Bobby glared at Jerry as his mother said, "Who are you? Is something wrong with my son?"

"Mrs. Pierno, I'd like to tell you my name, but considering your brother-in-law's...um, line of business, it's better that I keep that information to myself. Believe me, though, I'm calling as a person concerned about the well-being of your son."

"What is it? What's wrong with my son?"

"Physically, your son is fine. He's unharmed. He—"

"Oh God, you're playing mind games on me. Put him on the phone right now. Right this *second*. I demand that you put him on the phone."

"I can't do that."

"Damn it, you don't know who I am."

"Yes, I do. You're the mother of a son who came to my village with the intent to kill a man."

"You lying bitch, you—"

Rosa hung up.

She looked at the others, her head up, daring them to say anything. "She'll call back," she said.

Small nods agreed with her. Bobby scowled. "You don't know my mom. You'll have to hang up on her a lot more before she calms down."

"You don't know *me*," she said and heard her voice ring out.

The phone rang again.

And rang.

And rang.

And went to voice mail.

Bobby's mother swore and hung up.

Her hands curled into tight fists, Rosa stared at the cell phone in her hand, willing it to ring again. When it did, her shoulders relaxed.

She let it ring three times before picking it up. "Mrs. Pierno, if you swear at me or raise your voice, I promise I'll hang up, and you might never hear from your son again."

"Why, you—"

She hung up.

Two seconds later, it rang again. She let it ring twice more before picking it up. "This is your last chance to listen to me. Your son is in the room. Any abusive language and that will be the last thing your son will hear you say."

"Tell me," Gina Pierno's voice shook. "Tell me what's going on with Bobby. It's Dario, isn't it? His stepdad told me he ran away to see his father."

"This is nothing to do with Dario. This is about your son and the reason he came here. I'm a mother. I know what you must be feeling right now. And I know you didn't want your beloved baby son to grow up to be a killer."

"He's not a killer."

"He came here to kill a man. That was his intent."

"It was wrong. If I'd known... But no one told me." Her voice rose. "No one! I'm so angry at Bobby. I'm angry at my...at *everyone*."

"I'm glad you're angry. That shows you're a good mother. A good woman."

"I am! Now will you tell me? Do I have to beg?"

"Your son was caught by...local citizens." As the last second, she decided not to name the constable. If the Mafia came, she didn't want them to go looking for Jerry. And if it came to anyone's ears, the FBI or the ATF or whatever agency cared about stuff like that, she didn't want to involve Jerry. This was not the legal way to handle an attempted murder. And since they'd chased Bobby when he was just walking down Main Street, the only thing they could get him on would be carrying a weapon without a license.

"Is he in jail? Is that what you called to tell me?"

"Not real jail," Rosa said.

"What the hell—"

"Remember, no swearing." Rosa spoke with her mom voice that she used when she was displeased. The one that said she wasn't taking any backtalk.

"Okay, okay." The words sounded strangled, and it clearly wasn't okay, but Rosa wasn't going to quibble over a tone of voice.

"Luckily the citizens caught him before he shot anyone. And perhaps it's lucky for you that they don't want to give him to the police."

"You mean they're going to let him go?"

"You know better than that, Mrs. Pierno. If that were the case, I wouldn't be calling. No, the intent was to keep your son from attempting to kill a man who's become part of our community. The man we call Mo came to our village last summer. In that short time, he has revitalized a business that was limping along and made it a meeting place for the community. A place for young and old to go for family dinners and entertainment. He's given the village employment and enjoyment."

He'd certainly done both with her, she thought, and had to fight a giggle as a long breath came through the phone.

"In case you're interested," Gina Peirno's voice was sharp as a saw blade, "his real name is Vince Moretti, and he's known as Mo here, too. I never thought much of him and wasn't surprised when he betrayed us. But I gotta admit, since he left, his restaurant hasn't been the same."

"Then you know why we don't want him to leave. We thought you would like to talk to your brother-in-law about this."

There was no reply from the other end. But it was a live silence, not a dead one. Rosa raised her eyebrows. "I know you want your son back," she said quietly. "We're a very tight community, and a decision was made that if your brother-in-law agrees to stop his vendetta against Mo, we'll release your son."

Bobby made a protesting sound that ended in a yelp. Rosa didn't have to look at him to know that Jerry somehow made him shut up. She didn't turn around, didn't want the distraction. And she for sure didn't want that picture in her mind as she talked to Bobby's mom.

"Release my son from where?" Mrs. Pierno asked, her voice rose in volume and pitch. "Is he in jail?"

"I told you, not a real jail."

"What the fu—" Gina Pierno stopped, harsh breaths coming over the phone. "Okay, okay, I'm—"

"Mom, I'm here!" Bobby shouted. "I'm— Oof!"

"I'll call you back." Rosa hung up as Bobby screamed, "No! Put her back on. Put her back on! Let me talk to her."

He struggled with Jerry, half standing and squirming and trying to kick him and push him away with his cuffed hands. Jerry made a frustrated grunt, and as Mo stepped up to help him, he slammed Bobby down into the chair.

"Damn you," Bobby said with a sob. Tears glittered in his eyes, and his face contorted in a silent cry that made him look younger than his age. "Damn all of you."

"Damn you, you asshole, for trying to kill my father." Dario jumped to his feet and kicked Bobby in his shin.

"Ouch!" Bobby looked shocked. "It was business."

"It wasn't business, you fuckin' idiot. It's my father!"

"I didn't *want* to kill him."

"But you were going to. How would you like it if I killed your dad?"

"I would say good riddance. My dad is a piece of shit."

Dario glared at him. "Well, my dad isn't."

They stared at each other for a moment, their tension and emotion so strong that Rosa didn't want to breathe, and then all the angry energy seemed to whoosh out of Bobby, his tense posture wilting, his head drooping. "I'm sorry," he muttered. "Sorry."

"Yeah, you're one sorry asshole," Dario muttered back. Sniffing, he went back to his chair.

Still standing, Jerry jerked his thumb up. "C'mon, we'll wait in the outer office."

"I'll be good now." Bobby looked at him with all of the sullenness gone, leaving just unhappiness.

"Prove it by getting up."

Bobby stood.

Jerry looked at Dario. "And you." He jabbed his index finger in the air at Dario. "You sit and don't get up until we're gone. You understand?"

Dario nodded, looking as miserable as Bobby. As Jerry shepherded Bobby into the waiting area outside, Dario stared after them.

Next to him, Mo looked equally unhappy.

"Two out of three," Rosa whispered to herself as she picked up the cell phone and pressed redial.

In the next few minutes, she was going to see if she could make two out of three happy.

Plus 634 villagers.

35

Rosa felt all eyes on her as she pressed the Mom call number again. As she'd often done during her marriage, Rosa reminded herself of who she was as she pressed the speaker button. She was a strong woman. She was an excellent cook. She was a good mother and a woman with passion that she carried into everything she did. Cooking, friendship, love and—what mattered most right now as Gina Pierno answered the phone—being a mom.

"Hello again, Mrs. Pierno. May I call you Gina?"

"No. Yes. I don't care. How is my Bobby? I want to talk to him."

"Gina, you can talk to him, but only after we work a few things out."

"I know what you want. The same thing everyone wants from me." Her voice was as bitter as a bad fruit. "Especially men. You want access to Leo."

"I want access to your sister, Mrs. Leo Di Luca. Convince her to intercede on Bobby's behalf." She was silent for a few seconds and so was Gina on the other end. She felt encouraged. At least Gina hadn't automatically rejected her idea. Now she had to convince Gina that if she wanted Bobby safe, she needed to do just what she said. "Your role is important. You're the in-between person."

"What if I don't goddamn want to be in-between anything? I'm not a damn sandwich."

Rosa held back a laugh. This was not the time. But at least Gina had kept her sense of humor, though it had a bitter edge, too. She wondered if everything Gina did had that edge, the poison bleeding through. If so, she pitied her twice over.

"I thought you cared for your son," she said.

There was a silence, then Gina asked, "What happens if I don't do what you say?" Her voice was flat. The anger gone. She sucked in a breath, the gusty sound caught by the speakerphone. "What will you do to Bobby?"

"It depends on what happens on your end. Whether more people come after Mo. It's our objective to prevent that."

"You won't murder him. I can tell you're not that kind of people."

"I'm not. But others... They don't have the reverence for life that you and I have. Especially when they drink. And the people who live here, they like Mo. They like him a lot. They don't know your Bobby, but he came here to kill Mo, and they don't like that one bit." She lowered her voice. "Some of these men and women are farmers. They love their cows, their pigs, their chickens, their rabbits. But when the time comes, they kill them. They even eat them. If they can kill and eat an animal they love... Well, let's just say that your son's hairstyle and the jacket with the fur collar didn't endear him to the men in the village."

Gina groaned. "He wore that jacket? I told him it looked like he was carrying a dead animal around his neck."

"You're a woman of discernment."

Gina's laugh was broken. "The young can't help experimenting. When I was his age, I wore dresses that barely covered my ass."

"I bet on you they looked fabulous."

There was silence on the other end of the connection.

"You're just saying that because you want me to talk to my sister."

"You're going to talk to your sister for your son. Not because of anything I say to you. You love him, and you'll do it because you'll do anything you can to insure that he'll come back to you unharmed."

"Let me talk to him, and I'll do it."

Rosa knew this would come. If it were her, she'd insist too. "I'll call you back."

As she clicked off, Earl was pushing himself out of the chair. Something creaked, and Rosa wasn't sure if it was the chair, the floor, or Earl.

"Good girl," Earl said. "I knew you'd do it."

Rosa nodded, her muscles limp. It worked; it had really worked.

That meant there was a chance for Mo to live openly and peacefully. For his son to see him without repercussions. Perhaps even live with him.

As for her relationship with Mo... Her stomach tied into knots, and she couldn't think of it. Not now.

When this was over...if it ended well...then she would decide what to do.

"They're locking Bobby in a basement?" Mo sat on the edge of the old, brown recliner in his office, holding his hands to his head, as if keeping his hair from blowing off along with the top of his skull like in a cartoon.

"A basement won't hold Bobby," Dario said. "He's not as dumb as he looks."

"No one could be that dumb," Mo said. "What was he thinking when he got dressed this morning? He certainly didn't impress any of the locals."

"The basement is perfect." Rosa wanted to laugh but

didn't think Mo would appreciate it. She could see he was torn about this whole mess. He was always so strong and solid, talking to everyone yet never giving away anything about himself. In a village that had no secrets, he'd kept his for nearly eight months until it came looking for him in the form of two young men. One with love, the other with murder.

But now it felt to her that he carried his emotions on his skin instead of in a secret, locked-in place.

She wanted to think the change started before that, with her. But she wasn't going to ask him. All she knew for sure was that after she found out about the truth of the secret Mo had kept, it hadn't surprised her. Not really. At some level she'd known he was keeping something important hidden.

But if Mo was out of her life... Her breath exhaled in a gust that sounded harsh in the office with just the three of them.

With a slam only heard in her mind, she shut down that line of thought. She couldn't think of it right now.

"Why is the basement perfect?" Dario asked.

"Because of three reasons," she said. "Chad Schilling set it up for his brother, who was an addict. It's just a bedroom with a small bathroom. There's nothing valuable in it, just a small, thirteen-inch TV that doesn't even get cable. It's old and clunky, and I don't even know if it has color. And he has an extra strong lock on the door that kept Brad from sneaking out."

Mo stared at her, and she shrugged. "True. On Brad's request."

"Bobby will hate it." Dario's laugh came out like falling rocks.

"He won't hate all of it," Rosa said, and Mo chuckled.

"Why?" Dario looked from her to the other.

She just shrugged. "Some things men never hate."

"He has two nubile daughters," Mo said. "The Schillings are known for their...unusual voices and their blond looks. The daughters will be delivering food to him. I can guarantee Bobby won't resist them."

"If they're that hot," Dario said, "the wife will probably bring the food herself."

Rosa shook her head. "No, she trusts them. They took the chastity pledge at school."

"You're kidding," Mo said. He and Dario had the same wide-eyed look.

"Not at all. Taking the pledge is in fashion now. Their mother's very proud of them."

"I'm sure she is," Mo said. Then he and Dario shared the same look, as if they'd popped a candy into their mouth and found out if was sour.

Then they burst into laughter. She waited, her arms crossed. Only men would find chastity funny—until it got in their way. Then she suspected it wouldn't be so funny.

Mo's laughter stopped first, and the look he gave Rosa—the yearning and the heat and the need for her—made her heart skip and her breath catch and her skin warm. She uncrossed her arms and put her hands on the arms of the blue chair to hold herself back from pushing out of the chair and rushing to his side.

But when this was all over...

If it went the right way...

She jerked her gaze away from him. Too many ifs and buts. And she'd found out already that she couldn't plan for the best and the worst things in life. The moment she tried, it turned into chaos. She already had enough of that and didn't need more.

"What are you thinking?" Mo asked.

She gave a smile she knew didn't reach near her eyes.

But it was either smile or cry. "I was thinking we need a miracle."

He leaned forward and took both her hands in his, though he had to be aware that Dario was staring at them.

"I've already gotten my miracle."

She stared into his burning eyes that made her sad and happy at the same time, and she gripped his hands tightly, wishing she would never have to let go.

The next second, he released her hands. She stood and said she was going to see the kittens, and he let her walk away.

But just as she reached the door, the phone in her pocket rang. She stopped, pulled it out. No name showed on the display screen, only a phone number with a New Jersey area code.

"Who is it?" Mo asked, and she heard footsteps.

Keeping her back to Mo and Dario, she put the phone to her ear and said hello.

No one said anything for a moment, then a brusque male voice with a Jersey accent demanded to speak to Mo. The tone was of a man who was used to giving orders...and used to having them obeyed.

Tiny hairs rose on the back of Rosa's neck. She pressed the speakerphone button. "Who is this, please?" she asked, her voice cool, imagining she was the receptionist of a celebrated chef who kept turning down billionaires who wanted him as their personal chef, and the caller was someone trying to get him to be a guest on his puny cooking show.

"He'll know who it is. Put him on now."

She made a face and handed it to Mo. Obviously the caller wasn't playing her game. She would see how he felt after they made him play the village's game.

The thought made her shiver. Because it wasn't a game. Far from it. For Mo, it was life...

Or death.

36

"Leo." Mo heard the flatness in his tone. "It's been a while."

"You know why," Leo said.

"And you know why. Carl was my cousin."

"Carl was my friend. But he stole from me."

"You didn't have to—"

"Nothing. I didn't have to do anything," Leo said, and Mo heard a thump, as if he'd slammed his fist on a desktop, this former friend who'd sent a man to kill him.

But he wasn't dead. He was alive and happier than he'd ever been in Jersey. Happier, he believed, than Leo was with all his power.

The anger inside him deflated like a popped balloon. "In an odd way, Leo, it's good to hear your voice."

There was silence on the other end.

"I mean it." Mo put a hand to his chest, though Leo couldn't see him. "It's that Jersey voice. People talk different here."

"Ya think? Gotta say, I wouldn't mind the difference in the voice that answered. She look as good as she sounds?"

Mo lifted his eyes to Rosa and felt his chest expand. "Better."

A bark of laughter brought his attention back to the phone and away from her raised eyebrow. He sat straight, the soles of his shoes on the worn wooden floor. "You heard from Gina?"

"Jackie insisted I listen to her. Gina talked to some woman who wouldn't give her a name, but Gina swears that she's legit. Ya know, Gina's pretty good on nailing who's legit or not. Except for the men in her life. Those, she makes the wrong choice every fucking time."

"Yeah, I know."

"She's always been a drama queen."

"I know."

"So I'm not getting shook up about her dramatics, but she talked to Jackie and her ma, and they're all on my back. Not about you. You they don't give a shit about. It's all about baby Bobby, the fuck-up."

"Yeah, did you see the jacket he wears? It's got a fur collar."

"No shit. He wore that fucking jacket there? What a fucking asshole."

"And his hair... I'm surprised you can breathe the air in Jersey with all the hair spray the kids must use. You could've put a palm tree in the middle of Main Street and it would've stuck out less."

"What can I say? The kid takes after his dad. Like I said, a fuck-up."

"I guess I should thank you for sending him here."

"Hey, maybe it's one of those Freudian slips. My subconscious didn't really want you to disappear."

Mo wondered if Leo was seeing a therapist, but it wasn't something he was going to ask him. "Hope you keep that in your conscious mind, too."

"I like you, Mo. Always did."

"Same here. Until Carl. I went a little crazy," he said, not quite saying he was sorry but inferring it. He liked his life here. He wanted to stay in Miracle. Live his life in peace without worrying that someone was hunting him down like he was a five-point buck and it was the first day of deer hunting.

"You apologizing, Mo?"

Mo looked at his son. Dario was staring at him, watching his face to see his reactions. Unmoving. Unblinking. The muscles of his face pulled tight. As if he were afraid to breathe in case he'd miss something.

Mo shifted his gaze to Rosa, standing by the door with her eyes somber, her lips pressed together in a line. Then she realized he was staring at her, giving her all his attention. Her lips curved up, and her face grew soft. And her smile and her tenderness made his heart melt a little.

"Yes, I apologize." He enunciated each word clearly. "I was...crazed after Carl disappeared."

"I'm not saying I had anything to do with that," Leo said. "For all I know, Carl's in Vegas, blowing someone else's money there. You know he had a problem."

Mo nodded. He knew. And so did Leo. He shouldn't have put Carl in a position where he would steal. For all he knew, Leo did it on purpose to see if Carl could be trusted. A test Carl had failed.

"I'm not God," Mo said. "I'm not in the business of judging people."

There was silence on the end, and Mo waited about twenty seconds before Leo spoke in his rusty voice. "That's the difference between us. I am in that business."

"I don't envy you."

"You never did. That's why I always liked you. I'm glad we worked this out."

"Me too." Mo believed everything Leo said. Almost. "So you accept my apology? We're on the square?"

"Sure. On the square."

Leo's throwaway acceptance raised doubts that played a fast ping-pong game in his head, hitting the ball between the *is he lying?* side and his *I believe him* side.

The ball stuck in the middle. In the *prove it* zone.

"Glad that's settled," Leo said. "So, when are you

sending Bobby back? It'll be good to have Gina stop riding me. You know how anxious women get."

"I know." Mo looked at Rosa as he spoke. She watched him, her full lips curving slightly, sending encouragement, her dark eyes serious. He knew she wouldn't be carefree until this was over.

And it wasn't over yet.

Especially since he was about to make Leo an offer he could sure the hell refuse.

But if he'd learned anything in the last three years—and especially in the last three weeks—if a man never tried, then the man would never get lucky.

He smiled at Rosa, and her eyes turned smoky.

And sometimes, if he did try, the man would get very lucky.

"So I'll tell Manny to get the plane tickets," Leo said, "and he'll call you to let you know the details."

Mo sat up. In the last few minutes, he'd gotten too relaxed. Sometimes relaxation could kill a guy. "I've got a better idea."

"Oh?" Leo loaded that word with displeasure.

"I think if we'd talked this over in the beginning, face to face, it would've been over a long time ago."

"You wanna come back with Bobby? Sure. What about your kid? He wants to come back, too? Hell, I'll tell Manny to buy tickets for all of you."

"No." As he said the word, he could feel the disbelief on the other end, the shock. Or maybe that was just from the horror in Dario's face and the frown of concern on Rosa's. The way she stood so still.

Then she nodded. Her lips curving again. Giving him encouragement.

His tension eased. "How about if you come here?"

"You better be joking."

"Leo, it's no joke. It's my life."

"I'm only talking to you because you've got my nephew. You apologized, and I accepted it. You're asking too much."

"I'll pay for your plane tickets."

"I don't give a shit about the price of the plane tickets. I'm not feeling the respect. I gave you my word. You don't trust my word?"

"Leo, you tell me to my face, and I'll trust anything you say."

"I'll give you one second to change your mind. Five seconds to tell me you're sending Bobby back today. That five seconds starts right now."

Desperation twisted up inside him, closing his throat. Freezing his brain cells. Five seconds. No, four, three—

Rosa moved, taking Dario's hand. Dario clasped it. "The restaurant," she whispered. "We'll give him a feast in his honor."

"The village will give a feast in your honor."

There was silence on the other end, and then laughter poured into his ear. Hearty, knee-slapping laughter.

Mo closed his eyes, his shoulders relaxed, and held the phone toward his son and the brilliant, beautiful woman he was so lucky to have as a friend and lover.

The laughter slowed, and he brought it back to his ear.

"Good try," Leo said, still chuckling. "But no full house. You'll have to do better than that."

"Leo, I—"

"No excuses. It's yes or no. And if it's no, my sister-in-law won't be happy, my mother-in-law won't be happy, my wife won't be happy. And I sure the fuck won't be happy. To get me to goddamned snowy Wisconsin, it will have to be better than good. It will have to be spectacular. I know what you got, and except for the restaurant you no longer own, you ain't got shit."

"You're wrong."

"I'm not talking about your little karaoke place. That's nothing."

Leo was wrong there, too, but Mo wasn't offering him Mo's Place. "The restaurant in Jersey, that's still mine."

"Nah, it's Theresa's. She hired George Aubrey to manage it."

"Shit, no wonder you're complaining. Well, they better be ready to hand it over to you, because that's the one thing I kept in my name. Ask my lawyer. Ed Costanza. I'll call and give him permission to send it to you."

"You're shitting me."

"No. It was part of the prenup. Theresa had money from her grandma, and she kept that. My dad had already given me the restaurant, and I kept that."

There was a moment of silence.

"Well, shit. The restaurant ain't doing so good."

"You can fix it. Hire a good head chef. Give Bobby a job washing dishes."

Laughter roared out of Leo and went on and on. The kind that had tears and a hurt stomach and even drool. And while Leo was laughing, Rosa bent over and kissed Mo hard on the mouth. Not a lover's kiss. A congratulations kiss. Then Mo got up, holding the phone, and he kissed Dario hard on the mouth.

Leo's laughter slowed until his breath heaved. After one last heave, he said, "I'll talk to my lawyer. He'll probably tell me I have to pay you something."

"Put it in Dario's name."

"You're a mensch, Mo. A real mensch. That's how you got into this fuck-up."

"I know, and I don't care. You're coming then?"

"I'm coming to goddamn Wisconsin. Gina will want to come, too."

"Bring her."

"A couple others."

"Let me know how many. I'll have the feast ready."

"You're going to do this for everyone in the village?"

"I can't fit the whole village in here at once. I'll figure out a way to make it work. You can think of them as your food testers."

More chuckles came over the phone. "You're killing me with laughter."

"The second best way to go."

More laughter shouted out. "I don't know what's in the air there, but you were never this funny in Jersey."

Mo looked at Dario and then Rosa. His gaze stayed on her beautiful face, and he knew it wasn't the air. Just this one woman.

They hung up, and he hugged both of them. He was smiling and couldn't stop, even though it wasn't over yet. Even though anything could happen.

The thought made him tense inside, because he wanted this so much. It was so close, and if this fell apart—

"Mo," Rosa said. "You did it. You did it."

"Yeah, Dad." Dario beamed. "You did it!"

"I was going to leave you the restaurant. You lost it."

"I found my dad again. That's more important."

He blinked back tears. "Dario, Rosa, let's get ready to prepare a feast."

37

"No one's dead," Rosa told her oldest over Skype. Dario had set up the computer in Mo's office so she could see her son's handsome face as they talked. He looked like her father, she thought, a man she'd adored.

"Alive is always a good outcome," Matt said. "I'll use that line the next time the chef says my food isn't up to par."

High-pitched laughter came from Matt's background, one of his roommates, another student at the New York culinary school Matt attended, and the downside of Skyping. His roommate could hear everything she said. She'd have to be careful.

"So what's this text about me helping to prepare a feast?"

"Mo wants to thank the villagers for all they've done. It's..." Emotion clogged her throat. She stopped to swallow and take a deep breath to cool her warm cheeks. "It was wonderful the last time they got together to help Trish and Gunner. And now this..."

"I wish I could've been there," he said.

"Me too." She missed her oldest. It hurt to know he wasn't coming back to Miracle after he got his diploma, but she understood his ambition and would not make him feel any guilt. She would not be an anchor that stopped him from accomplishing his dreams.

"Mo's going to have a hell of a time finding a place to hold a feast for over 600 people," Matt said. "I don't know where it would be."

She shook her head. She'd been thinking about that.

"He should wait until spring. You can do it outdoors at Miracle Lake."

"He doesn't want to wait," she said.

"No one wants to wait. But everyone has to."

"You're cheery."

"You want something cheery? I can send you the YouTube link of a dog chef."

"A dog? Any resemblance to your dad?"

The roommate laughed, and so did Matt. She grinned, feeling better. "Okay, I'll tell Mo what you said."

"He could give everyone a free dinner. It doesn't have to be a feast."

"I know. But he wants to prepare a feast for the village. He's got an idea in his mind." She liked the idea, too. She could see it. Only, every time she did, it was like a feast in Italy, outside somewhere. Long tables. People laughing. Children playing.

Just the way they would do it at Miracle Lake.

"It's not the only feast he's planning," she said.

"What's that?"

"It's a smaller one. For someone...special." She wasn't mentioning names, not with the roommate in earshot. "He'll be flying in with a few friends."

Matt sat up straight. "From New Jersey?"

She nodded. "He has about a dozen dishes planned. I don't know how we'll do it all. Scotty and the part-time line cook mostly do bar food. I'm the one that does the Italian food. Mo can cook, but he'll be busy being the host."

"I can come and cook."

"Really?" Hope welled up in her. "How?"

"Plane. I can't miss something like that."

"I'll pay for your tickets."

"No, you've done enough. I know how to get the

money."

"From your dad?"

"I was thinking of Tony."

"Tony? Don't borrow money from him for this. You're doing my...boss a favor. I'll pay."

"You worry too much. I'm not borrowing from Tony. He owes me."

"Really? How so?"

He snickered at the camera. "Never mind."

She looked straight at the camera and gave it The Stare. Making sure he saw it.

"The Stare doesn't work long distance," he said. "Besides, I'm getting too old to be cowed by it."

She put a hand to her heart. "It's awful when a superpower no longer works."

He laughed again. "I've gotta go. It's been good talking to you. Call me when you have the date set. Tell Mo I'll email him about the menu."

She nodded. "Love you, sweetie."

"Love you back, Mama Mia."

The picture blanked out, and the big smile froze on her face then melted off.

Even telling herself she was the luckiest woman in Miracle—when not too long ago she'd thought she was the unluckiest—didn't bring the smile back.

Now she could tell Mo that Matt would come. She could tell him about Matt's idea of having the bigger village feast by Lake Miracle when it was warmer. The two churches in town could bring tables. Or everyone in town who had folding tables and chairs could bring them. Mo could supply everything else.

She still sat, though, her body as lethargic as her emotions. Because after she told him that, she would have to do one more thing: Pack up her clothes, bring them to the other apartment and start cleaning.

Too many people knew about her and Mo and expected something more. *No.* She needed to be honest with herself. If necessary, brutally honest. She was starting to expect something, but there was nothing to expect. The sex she and Mo had...it was just something that happened. Something wonderful. Something fabulous. But in the end, it was just a man and a woman having sex.

That's it. Sex. Fuck buddies. From the beginning, that's what she'd said it would be. Mo was the kind of man who wouldn't want to hurt her. He was...honorable. After Mike, Mo had been just what she needed. Like chicken soup for a cold, Mo was her chicken soup.

They'd been thrown together, they liked each other, and they did what adults do on occasions like that.

It would be easy to fantasize that it was more, but it couldn't be anything else. Mo never expected her to feel anything more. And she certainly never expected it of him.

Now his son was here, and it looked like he was staying.

She was glad for Mo. Glad for both of them. Fiercely glad.

And she was glad it happened before she got too used to sleeping with him.

She stood. She needed to move her things out before he asked her to.

Feeling as if her shoes were made out of concrete, she headed toward the hall.

38

L ife went on, and so did the restaurant. Food was served, and the bar was crowded. Something was wrong with Rosa, but instead of Mo finding out what it was, he had to be out serving drinks. Smiling and celebrating and slapping other men on their backs. And they slapped him back. A man's way of showing affection.

But always in his mind was Rosa's wan face instead of her normally vivid, confident one. He remembered her after she'd found out about Mike's affair, so furious that he'd felt sparks coming off of her. She'd made him think of a warrior queen. He'd wanted to get down on his knees, tell her he'd do anything she said. For instance, if she wanted revenge sex, he'd be up for the job.

Now he wanted to hold her and kiss her face and tell her that whatever was wrong, he'd stand by her side. He'd hold her hand. He'd go through it with her.

But he couldn't get to her. He'd taken her son's advice and told everyone he was going to put together a feast for the village by Miracle Lake this spring or summer. He was posting a sheet by the bar. Anyone who had plans for any of the weekends should mark it down so he wouldn't pick that date. He wanted everyone to be there.

So instead of talking to Rosa, he was giving out two free drinks to everyone tonight. No more than two, because he didn't want anyone to do anything stupid.

Every time he said that, he got a laugh. Earl Raasch said, "Trying to stop stupid is like trying to stop weeds from growing."

He laughed back, but his heart was sore, and there would be no cure for the ache in his chest until he found out what was wrong with Rosa.

Had Mike called and said something to her? Mo wasn't a violent man, but in the last year, he'd wanted to slam Mike in his soft belly more than a few times.

Or was it something about one of her kids? That would bother her more than anything Mike did.

Her hours ended at ten tonight, and instead of sticking around, she'd disappeared. As usual, he needed to stay around until everyone left. More people had made it to the bar tonight to celebrate. Even the villagers he rarely saw had come for the free drinks. Everyone was on a celebratory high.

They'd done it! They'd helped save another villager from harm. It was a euphoric experience, and this made it twice in a year's time they'd done something extraordinary for a neighbor. It was truly a time to celebrate. And as the person whose ass was saved—and Mo very much liked having his ass right where it was—he wished he could be happier.

And he would be. As soon as he found out why Rosa had lost her fire. Once he knew, he could help her fix it, and they would both be happy again.

———————————

Closing time. Rosa peered out the front window in her darkened apartment, watching the last customers weave out. Their laughter drifted up to her. The light streaming out of the restaurant's front window blinked out, leaving only a glow from the dimmed lights Mo kept on all night.

Tonight it felt sad to look at it—the diminished light reminded her of her life—and she turned to gaze into the bedroom at the kittens cuddled in her bed. She'd turned off her lights, but her shades were up, and streetlight reached her window. She easily saw the kittens hugging each other, the sight making tears warm her eyes.

She blinked them back. She was not a young girl anymore. She had always known her affair with Mo was temporary.

She just hadn't thought it would be so wonderful.

Or that it would feel so right.

Of that she would want more than temporary.

But that was life, she told herself as she stood and closed the front curtains. She wanted to be in bed before Mo came upstairs.

In the twin-sized bed, she contorted her body so as not to bother the kittens. The apartment smelled like pine-scented all-purpose cleaner. Not a horrible smell but not the smell of Mo. He was musk with a slight underlay of garlic and basil and olive oil. She'd told him once during their lovemaking that he tasted good enough to eat.

Only that time he'd been the one to do the eating.

Heat flushed through her, and she pushed it away. Not tonight. Except for the kittens, this was going to be a cold body night.

Yes, she missed him. But it was okay. She would be fine without him. Right now she felt like the happy was sucked out of her, but it wouldn't be the first time she'd lost her happy. Or the first time she felt as if she would never find it again. But it came back before. It would come back again.

Hurried footsteps thudded on the steps, and she tensed. Dario was already in the apartment; she'd heard him come up about ten minutes after she did. It must be Mo hurrying down the hall.

She closed her eyes and clenched her hands into fists. This was so silly. She had no right to feel this way. They were just friends with benefits. Lovely, lovely benefits.

A mewl caught her attention, then a small and warm and furry body climbed up on top of her and curled up on her belly. She reached down to splay her hands against the small body. A knock came on the door, and she jerked her head up. Staring at the wall, as if she could see Mo through it.

Another knock came. She heard his breathing, though it was impossible. She heard his heart beat. It wasn't possible, either. Not within the human range of hearing.

But as she held her breath, another impossible thing happened. She could *feel* him pull back his fist from knocking again. *Feel* his stare at the door. *Feel* his shoulders slump. *Feel* him turn to his apartment.

And then she heard his footsteps on the hall floor as he headed to his apartment.

Her breath came out in a shudder.

I will be okay. I will heal. I will get through this. After all, it was just sex.

But not, she thought as she petted the kitten, sex as she'd ever had it before. With Mo, she'd been a woman on fire. And without him, the fire was just a pale spark.

39

Women. They were killing Mo by seconds.

Mo sliced onions as if they were the enemy. Better than taking his crazy emotions out on the next person who walked into his view.

First, that call from Theresa waking him this morning, demanding that he force Dario to fly back to Jersey. Then when he went to find Rosa, she was gone, still avoiding him. It was driving him crazy.

What had he done? He'd thought that after talking to Leo, everything would be perfect. He was reunited with his son, and no one was trying to kill him. But instead of being happy, he was as miserable as any lovesick teenager.

Love. That messed a man up faster than being caught in a giant Mixmaster.

There. He said it. Not aloud, but he'd admitted it to himself. Love. He *loved* Rosa. He'd fallen in love with her slowly. Of course he loved her looks. What man didn't? Even the few gay men he knew in Miracle noticed Rosa's body. And gay men could be a lot more specific and raunchy than straight men.

Every raunchy thing they said was a raunchy thing he'd thought.

But he'd had raunchy thoughts about women for many years, and that didn't make him love them. That just made him lust after them.

He slowed his slicing, thinking about Rosa's smile, the way she carried her head so high. The way she flirted with men almost unconsciously. A part of her Italian

DNA, along with her strength of character. And it was a part of his DNA to love that about her. To love everything about her.

Doubts crawled into his mind, and his slicing stopped completely.

He'd been there when she needed him. He was her boss, and he'd given her a helping hand, letting her stay in the apartment—only it had turned out to be a dump. After that, perhaps sleeping together was just...convenient for her. And maybe at some level, a way to get back at Mike.

The thought made him want to punch something, and he rejected it. Perhaps unconsciously she might have done it for that reason, but she had some feelings for him. He knew that. She was a passionate woman, and he knew she liked him. It wasn't just sex; he didn't believe that.

He should ask her about her feelings. But he dreaded it. If the words weren't spoken, he had hope. Once words were spoken...

"Hey, Dad."

"Hey, Dario." He tried to dredge up a smile, but it wasn't happening. "How's my boy?"

"Mom called me."

"You answered this time?" Theresa had been calling Dario since he got here, but he had his cell on buzz, and when he saw her name or the name of his stepfather, he ignored the call.

"She woke me up. I answered before I thought."

Mo showed his sympathy with a grimace. "She did the same to me this morning."

"She threatened to tell the authorities you're keeping me out of school. She said she won't let me stay with you."

Mo looked at the pile of onions on the prep table and pushed back the anger that was a black wave inside him. He imagined himself with muscles like a bodybuilder, with his hands up, holding that hot wave of blackness high above his head, keeping it from coming down on him.

"What are you doing?" Dario asked.

"Staying calm."

"That doesn't work." Dario shook his head like he was the wise man on top of the mountain. "Not with Mom."

Mo started scraping the onions into a bowl. "I'll call my lawyer and ask him to deal with it. If you're staying with me—"

"I am!"

"Good." Though a prickly ball of darkness still sat in the middle of his chest, he was happier than before Dario had walked in to dump this problem in his lap. He'd tell his lawyer to check out how Theresa had remarried so swiftly. And what she was doing with the money from the restaurant. Find out where it was going. "Don't worry. Ed will take care of it."

"You're sure?"

"It's the kind of thing he enjoys doing. I'll call the school and set up an appointment. I suppose you didn't bring your birth certificate."

Dario shook his head.

"And I'm using a different name." Mo shrugged. If he hadn't changed his name, he might not be alive and talking to his son. "The lawyers will figure it out."

Dario nodded, but his usual eager eyes looked dull. Just as dull as Mo felt.

"We'll work this out." He reached out and hugged Dario twice, though he was probably getting onion juice on his son's sweatshirt. "We got this far, didn't we? What happened here last night was—"

"A miracle."

Mo stared at Dario. Maybe it was a miracle. Or maybe it was just the villagers of Miracle.

"And you know I'm pretty smart," Dario continued. "If I miss school, I don't care. I'm smarter than most of them."

"You are missing school, and I do care. We had other things that took top priority, but now that I'm not wearing a target on my back, we have to fix this." He put his hand on Dario's shoulder. "Right now, my top priority is you."

And as he said that, Mo wondered if that was the reason Rosa had changed. Because she had to have known Dario was his top priority and not her.

Immediately images crowded in his head of the smile lighting up her face when she saw Dario. And the way she was with her own sons. She glowed when she was with Tony. She even glowed with the kittens.

No, the reason she changed her mind had nothing to do with Dario. Just him.

Last night, when she looked at him, she hadn't glowed anymore.

And his heart that had felt so happy and newly healed had started to crack into pieces again.

———

"Dad, Mrs. Di Luca is on the phone."

Sitting behind his desk in his office, Mo jerked his gaze up from the menu on his computer. He'd just changed the feast menu for the tenth time. When he'd proposed the feast to Leo, he'd thought he and Rosa would be planning it. But when he'd gone upstairs to look for her, she wasn't there.

And now Jackie Di Luca, the Don's wife, was calling him.

This day kept getting worse.

He held his hand out. "Thanks, Dario." Just saying his son's name and looking at his face improved his spirits. "You're still my favorite kid."

Dario grinned. "You're still my favorite dad. You want me to stay?"

Mo shook his head. Why make both of them suffer? Besides, Jackie was a friend of Theresa's, and he didn't have a good feeling about this.

Damn it, couldn't anything be easy?

Reaching for the phone, he pushed down the self-pity. Life wasn't easy for a lot of people, but they didn't give up, and neither did he.

"Jackie, it's been a while."

"Mo, I missed you," she said, her loud voice like a bullhorn. "The restaurant hasn't been the same since you left. I can't believe you're in friggin' Wisconsin. If you had to go somewhere, why not someplace warm? Theresa was sure you'd go to Florida."

Mo's eyes aimed toward the desktop. Not looking at Dario, who remained in the room, rubbing his chin, his forehead wrinkled. With Jackie's loud voice, Dario had to have heard what she said. He probably didn't want Mo to see in his eyes what he was thinking. That Dario's mom had told Jackie where she thought Mo was because she wanted Jackie to tell Leo. She wanted Mo killed and out of the way so she could remarry Tommy in the Catholic Church.

"Leo said we were invited to dinner," Jackie said. "I told him he's crazy, but he just looked at me. You know the way he does."

"I've seen that look." The look that sized him up for a

coffin.

"Besides, Gina would moan if we didn't go and bring back her fuck-up son. So I looked at the weather; we sure don't want to go during a snowstorm and be stuck there. Sunday looks good weather-wise, and it works for Leo. So that's when we'll be there. That okay with you?"

"It's good." He wanted to get this over with. Besides, he couldn't keep Bobby locked up forever, though Chad Schilling said he wasn't even trying to get out and wasn't giving his daughters any trouble. Probably because both girls knew how to handle a weapon. His oldest had gotten the biggest buck in the village during the hunting season. The second oldest had caught her boyfriend cheating on her, and rumor was she'd thrown him over his sports car, and he'd landed on a pile of dog shit. If Mo were locked in their basement, he wouldn't defy them either.

"Theresa's coming with us, too. I told her you'd be happy to see her."

Mo's shoulders tensed, but he resisted the impulse to jolt up straight. He gripped the phone so tightly the plastic dug into the bones of his hand. "Just a second."

Putting his hand over the phone, he smiled. "Dario, could you get me a mug of coffee? I need some caffeine to get me through this." He put the phone to his ear but waited until Dario left the room before he said, "No."

"Mo, don't give me any crap. You have to—"

"I don't have to do shit. She lied to me, and she lied to my son. I won't do it."

"You have to. Leo will—"

"Leo will do nothing. I'll call him and tell him straight out what happened."

There was two seconds of silence before she talked again. "Theresa said you'd say that. She wants to talk to

Dario. If you let her come, she promises to give Dario written permission to live with you."

"You tell Theresa I'm calling my lawyer about her."

"Theresa knows lawyers. Hell, she's married to one of the best. You pit one lawyer against another, and by the time they wrap it up, Dario will be old enough to graduate from college."

He exhaled and inhaled slowly. Damn it, she was right. "I don't trust her promises. It wouldn't be the first that she broke. She made me promise never to try to divorce her, and then I find out she must've talked to the lawyer before I got out of Jersey. Hell, maybe long before that."

A laugh came from the other end, Jackie finding this subject amusing.

Well, why the hell not?

"Tell me," he said, "she was sleeping with Tommy long before I left, right?"

"Mo, I can't talk about this. It's not right to ask me."

"You just told me the answer right there. She lied to keep me from finding a new chance of happiness. She knew I'd keep my word."

Another moment of awkward silence came over the phone. He looked at the door. Dario should be coming back soon, and he needed to end this. He leaned forward, opening his mouth to—

"You know how she is," Jackie said. "You shouldn't be surprised. She's not a bad person. She's just...selfish." She paused and, when Mo didn't jump in, said, "Okay, she can be a bitch. But she's not all bad. She can be entertaining."

Mo shrugged. Theresa's attempts to entertain him had stopped a long time ago. Not that he'd blamed her, considering the long hours he worked. It wasn't as if he'd been the perfect husband.

But he'd never stolen from her. He'd never lied about something important. He'd never cheated on her. He'd never—

Clenching his left hand, he stopped the self-pity, the anger. Shut it down. He needed to go forward not backward. "Bring her along. Tell her I expect her to keep her promise."

"What about..." A huff came from Jackie's end. "You know who?"

"Husband Number Two? She can bring him. Bring 'em all. Any ghosts from my Christmas past you want to bring, too?"

"Huh? Oh, I get it." She laughed again. "No ghosts. Just live people."

"You might warn Theresa that Dario hates Tommy. She brings him, Dario won't be happy to see her."

"Good idea. That's nice of you to warn her."

"I'm not doing it for her. I'm doing it for Dario."

"You're a good dad, always were. I'll see you on Sunday. Anything I should bring from Jersey?"

"Just your appetite."

He hung up. With Dario here, there was nothing he wanted in Jersey. Everything else he wanted was right here in Miracle.

Rosa. She was here. Pictures of her flashed in his mind. Preparing food. Her swaying walk. Laughing. Serious. With her sons. Without them. Playing with the kittens. In his bed. Her face languorous from lovemaking, her skin glowing. The most beautiful sight he'd seen in his life.

The sound of footsteps in the hall made him blink away the images, and he sat up straight as Dario stepped into the office, a pie box in one hand, a mug of coffee in the other. "Sorry it took so long. The pie lady came in."

"Katie? She came earlier. I didn't notice a shortage."

"I asked her that, too." One crease lined his forehead. "She said this one is just for you."

He stood. "Did she say it was a Lucky Pie?"

Dario rolled his eyes. He didn't believe in Katie's talent of matching the right pie with the right person, which she said she was "compelled" to make and bring to the person who needed it.

But strange things happened in Miracle. So why not this?

Mo took the pie from him. "What name did she call this pie?"

Dario set the coffee down. "Comfort Pie."

Mo sank back into the chair, a big pit opening in his mind. That wasn't the pie name he'd been hoping for.

He sat straight. This couldn't be it. There had to be some way to change the next pie.

He glanced down at his notes on the meal. The dinner planning first. Only four days. He had to start that. After the feast was over, then he could concentrate on his life.

40

Mo was busy with his menus for the Jersey contingent as well as taking care of his regular diners, easily working twelve-hour days. No time for Rosa, which right now she didn't mind. Matt emailed her, letting her know he and Mo were exchanging emails and texts about the feast. He was catching a plane for a nonstop flight to Madison at an obscenely early hour on Saturday and expected to be in Miracle mid-day. His new roommate was coming with him. Rosa told him they could sleep in her apartment, sharing the bed while she slept on the couch.

She half expected him to text her that he was staying at his dad's place with the two unused bedrooms that shared a pass-through bathroom. But he never did, and she was happy that he'd rather stay at her cramped apartment than with his father.

At least *that* was going okay. And maybe Mike would eventually get it that his actions had repercussions.

Then it was late afternoon Friday. Sunday was only two nervous days away, and she was grabbing frozen ground pork from the walk-in freezer when she heard a footstep. She went still for a second, knowing who it was before she turned around and looked at Mo's tense face.

"What happened with us?" he asked.

"Nothing happened. It was..." She exhaled and looked down and then up. She couldn't avoid this anymore, and Mo deserved the truth. "Everything has changed."

"Everything always changes. But we can—"

"Do *nothing.*" Only the packages of fish kept her from

throwing her hands up. "We have family involved."

"Dario adores you."

"No, I adore *him*. He just likes me."

"Likes and respects. In a short time, he'll love you, too."

She frowned. "When we started this, it was just us. We were—"

"Don't say it."

"Friends," she said firmly. "We were good friends, and I found...comfort in your arms."

"More than comfort."

"Pleasure." She smiled, because it was impossible to do anything else with this melted-butter feeling sliding down into her belly.

"More than pleasure," he said, his eyes gleaming, and the melted-butter feeling slipped lower inside her....

She shifted the packages to her left arm and held out her right arm, warding him off. "I don't deny it. But things have changed. Your son is here. The *Mafia* is coming. And then this thing between us..."

"This wonderful thing."

She laughed shakily. She couldn't deny it any more than she could deny her heart was beating too fast. "Yes, it's wonderful. But everything happened so fast, and I think for now I need to...pull back. Slow down. No decisions. When this is over, maybe then we can decide what we want to do."

"I'll step back and wait, but I already know what I want." His eyes burned. "I know with my heart."

Then he snapped around and marched out, leaving her standing in the freezer until she realized her skin was prickling as if ice crystals were digging into her pores. With a shiver, she headed out, her arms full of cold meat and her mind full of uncertainty.

———————

Saturday already. It seemed to Rosa that every moment since Mo had stalked out of the walk-in freezer had been an eternity. And at the same time, each hour had flown. Now Matt and his roommate were in her apartment, and she laughed to see his roommate had golden brown hair that curled below her shoulders, was about five foot four, and looked at Rosa out of cool blue-gray eyes surrounded by long eyelashes.

Rosa grabbed Matt and hugged him hard. Then she let him go, turned to the roommate, and hugged her hard, too.

When she pulled away, she saw the coolness was gone, and instead a mix of insecure emotions shimmered on the young woman's face and in her eyes.

Rosa beamed at her then looked at Matt. "I should have asked your roommate's name."

"Zoe Brentwood." He slung his arm around Zoe's shoulders, not a friendly gesture, a possessive one.

"I'm happy to meet you." Rosa let her smile shine higher, sending Zoe the silent approval her mother-in-law had never bestowed upon her. "How generous that you came here to help cook."

"It was an offer I couldn't refuse," Zoe said, then she grinned up at Matt, who was looking at her with laughter and admiration in his face.

Rosa's eyes got misty, and she had to blink fast.

Her first baby was in love.

And he was loved back.

It warmed her heart. What she most wanted for her children was that they be happy. That their marriages wouldn't be unequal like hers with their father.

Marriage to Mo would be equal.

She sucked in her breath sharply.

"Something wrong, Mom?" Matt asked.

She started to shake her head then stared at him. "Nothing's wrong. Why would you think that?"

"Because you look as if someone conked you on the head with a hardball."

"Thank you for that lovely image." She walked backwards to the door. "I'll leave you two to unpack. Zoe, I'm sorry I'm leaving you with this barbarian. We'll talk later." She pointed at the bathroom. "I hope you like kittens. There are two in the bathroom. The boy is Checkers; the girl is Pie. You can let them out of the bathroom but not out of the apartment, please."

Then she whirled around to leave, the word *please* remaining in her mind. *Please, please, please.*

Only she wasn't sure what she was saying please about.

Maybe it was *please, don't let me do anything stupid.* Or *please, just let me be strong.*

Because right now she was feeling very, very weak.

41

Sunday

"I want to see Bobby right now." Gina Pierno stood inside the restaurant and glared at Mo as if he were the one who'd sauntered into the village with a sniper's rifle in his trunk.

After three years of looking at women who didn't have a plastic surgeon in the top five numbers of their phone directory, the faces of all three women—Gina, Jackie, and Theresa—looked odd. As if they were escapees from a wax museum.

"You don't need to worry about your son," Earl Raasch said, here to welcome the visitors as the president of the village board. "We're taking care of him just fine. He's even got a TV."

Gina stared at the older man wearing a Daniel Boone jacket. Earl stuck his chest out. "It's deer," he said.

"Deer?" Her nose wrinkled as if she could smell blood. This from a woman who, whether she knew it or not, lived off the blood of other people.

"My leather jacket." He lifted an arm, showing off the sleeve. "I do taxidermy and reupholstery at my shop. The jacket's made out of deer leather. A lot of folks just want the heads with antlers, you know. Or just the meat. When that happens, I have the skin tanned. This year, my associate and I bought our own tanning machine." He looked down at his jacket, the folds of his face settling in satisfaction. "I usually sell the skin but had this jacket made special for me."

"Your shop's near here?" Leo asked.

"You see the size of the village? Every place is near each other. Want a tour? It's an hour before the feast. I got an eight-foot brown bear in my living room."

"Leo," Gina's voice was sharp, "I want you to go with me to see Bobby."

The look he gave her was sharper than her voice, but she glared at him, obviously too stupid to be afraid of her brother-in-law. "You promised to make sure Bobby's all right. If I see something wrong and tell you, you won't believe me."

"That's true, Leo," Jackie said.

He gave Jackie a dark look, but she just smiled. He flattened his lips together, not saying anything. Mo had never heard Leo say a bad word about Jackie. Not even when he was with other women.

"I'll take you to see Bobby," Mo said. He glanced at Dario. His son had suffered a hug from Theresa with gritted teeth. She'd hung on to him for a minute longer than she should have, and he'd twisted out of her grip and stepped back. Her face had turned stony, her cheeks red. More, Mo guessed, because Gina and Jackie were watching than anything else.

Tommy wasn't here, after all. Mo didn't ask where he was because he didn't care. Two burly men rounded up the group. Enforcers acting as bodyguards for Leo. Mo had known both men before, and they greeted him like he was an old friend. He'd always gotten along with Leo's associates. In his restaurant, he'd gotten along with everyone. Part of his success. It was just his private life that he'd screwed up.

But he would worry about that later. He just needed to get through this.

"Ask Rosa to help out while I'm gone," he told Dario.

He'd asked her to greet everyone before they'd come, and she'd said she was busy. Matt and his girlfriend both said they could handle the prepping, but she ignored them.

A request from Dario would be different. Mo knew she wouldn't say not to Dario. She had a soft heart for him.

He followed Dario into the back, passing the kitchen to head to his office, forcing himself not to look at Rosa and feeling her not looking at him, which made him wonder if she felt him not looking at her.

He wanted to laugh at himself, with all these emotions churning inside him like he was a teenage girl instead of a grown man. He'd never felt like this over a woman before.

But he'd never felt as content and fulfilled as the short time they were together.

When he came out, zipping his jacket, he saw she was taking off her apron and saying something to Matt.

Good, she would be out in a moment.

He and the others left right away, not having much choice with Gina tapping the pointed toe of her high-heeled designer shoe, too impatient to wait for Dario to return. Arnie, one of the bodyguards, came with them. That made four in Mo's four-wheel-dirve SUV: Gina, Leo, Arnie, and himself. The drive was in silence except for comments on the snow that carpeted the grass and fields, though New Jersey was no stranger to snow.

The farmhouse was a half mile down the highway from the village, a white two-story house with green shutters and roof. Chad Schilling had built an addition in the back that had a family room plus a craft room for Nancy and his two attractive daughters.

Nancy let them in. A curvy woman on the heavy side with curly blond hair, she reminded Mo of a Germanic beer waitress. Wearing a sweatshirt and jeans, she gaped at Gina, who was dressed as if she was going to a charity benefit. Mo had to ask her twice to take them downstairs.

"We really like your son," Nancy said as she unlocked the door, and music traveled up to them. "He hasn't even tried to escape and is so polite. My daughter Sherry is with him right now. She's got such a soft heart." She glanced at Mo. "You know how she is."

Mo nodded, though he didn't know the teens that well. "Is she the daughter who won the 4H Blue Ribbon for her pig?"

"That's Brooke. Sherry was on the homecoming court. She's going to school to be a dental hygienist next fall." She beamed before leading them downstairs into the den of pounding music that made Mo wince.

He was the last one downstairs, but he heard Nancy gasp while still on the stairway. When he reached the basement, everyone was staring. Nancy had both hands pressed against her face. Gina's rubbery face was a mask of horror that wouldn't have looked out of place in an old Dracula movie. Leo and Arnie appeared to be holding back laughter, the effort turning Arnie's face red.

Mo turned in the direction of their stares, and he saw Bobby—much more of Bobby than he'd ever wanted to see. Stretched out on top of Sherry, he was pumping away to the music, her blond hair spread on the pillow and her long legs wrapped around the top of his thighs.

Mo snorted. Then he chortled. Then he bent forward and laughed.

As if that was the cue for everyone else to snap out of their shock, Nancy screamed, and Sherry started yelling.

Mo headed back up the steps, laughing so hard his stomach hurt. In the kitchen, he collapsed on a chair. Leo collapsed on the one next to him. Mo had been laughing so loudly he hadn't even heard Leo's steps behind him.

Leo grabbed a paper napkin out of the holder on the table. Still laughing, he wiped tears from his eyes. "I told Arnie to stay downstairs. In case anyone gets violent." He shook his head. "Jesus, it was worth coming here just for that."

Mo took a napkin and used it to blow his nose. "Glad we can entertain you. Wait'll you eat the food. You won't want to leave."

"Yeah, I will." Leo's laughter stopped. "This ain't for me." He swept his hand at the view out the window. Snow and land covered in snow, with just a few trees. A big barn in the back of the house, and a smaller one that Mo suspected the family used as a garage. "It's too quiet here for this Jersey boy. But you like it, don't you? I can see you do."

Mo nodded. Not feeling like laughing anymore.

"I was hoping you'd come back," Leo said. "If I liked what I saw, I was going to let everyone know you were okay. Bring the restaurant back into fashion."

"I appreciate that."

"But you like it here. You're not coming back, are you?"

Mo thought of Rosa. If she didn't want him, if what they had was just a fling, he would need to get away from her. To see her every day and not be with her, it would be like walking around with an open wound in his heart.

"I'll tell you by the end of the day, all right?"

As Leo nodded, Mo heard a fresh bout of yelling downstairs. Leo cracked up again, and Mo laughed, too, but with an ache in his chest.

After the dinner was over, he would make up his mind. Leave or stay.

42

Rosa was sitting at the table next to Mo for two reasons, neither of which made her happy. After the others came back, she'd gone back to the kitchen, expecting to stay until the dinner was done. But ten minutes later, Mo had marched into the kitchen and asked why she wasn't in front acting as hostess.

She'd told him she was cooking, though her chicken parmesan was in the oven, as Matt and Zoe had helpfully pointed out. When she'd replied that she was helping them, they'd rolled their eyes and insisted they didn't need her.

Maybe they didn't, but she wasn't leaving.

Her emotions were too mixed up right now to be with Mo. She wasn't sure what he wanted. And she wasn't sure what she wanted.

It wasn't a good place to be. She wouldn't make a good dinner companion. Not in front of the people she knew. And certainly not in front of a Mafia boss and Mo's ex-wife.

Not that she told Mo any of this. She just said no and gave him The Stare.

Mo left, but then Dario had come in.

And she still wasn't leaving.

And then Earl, amusement deepening the many lines in his face.

And she thanked him and said she was staying in the back.

And then Elsa, the minister of the metaphysical church that Rosa attended now. With her white-blonde hair and slender body, she was elegant in a blue dress that looked *haute couture*—another word for *expensive*. Which it could be, since she'd shown up nearly four years ago seemingly out of nowhere, reminding Rosa of a fairy godmother in a Disney movie.

Like the others, Elsa told Rosa that Mo sent her.

Rosa caved only because she didn't know who Mo would send next. Leo Di Luca? She wouldn't put it past him. Mo was not a man who gave in easily.

Elsa went upstairs with her to help her pick out a dress. She told Rosa that two of the Jersey ladies were wearing black and Dario's mother was wearing pine green.

With Elsa's urging, Rosa chose a dark red dress with long sleeves and a draped neckline. It clung to her hips and breasts. As she strode past the kitchen in her black heels, Scotty wolf whistled. When she and Elsa entered the dining room, everyone was seated already. Their heads swiveled to stare at her and Elsa. Following the advice her mother had given her when she was a teenager, she lifted her chin and pretended she was royalty.

There were only two seats left, and Elsa sat next to Sam at the end of the table before Rosa could. The only one left was in the middle of the long table, with her back to the front window, between Mo and Earl.

She was just in time for the meal. Brenda and the Tim the busboy headed in from the kitchen with trays loaded with antipasto platters.

"I'm glad you decided to make it," Mo said as Brenda began setting platters in front of the guests.

Rosa smiled and kicked his shin.

He jerked and made a garbled noise. Lisa brought Rosa a glass of red wine without waiting for instructions.

If she had waited, Rosa would've told her to bring the whole bottle.

"Perfect timing," Mo said, giving Rosa an intense glance.

She looked at him, and her breath caught in her throat. Then his gaze flicked away, and she exhaled. He introduced her to Leo Di Luca, a swarthy man about her age with a Roman nose. He carried some extra weight, though she'd never call him fat. Especially not to his face. He greeted her with an approving nod, and his eyes gleamed, as if he could see her naked.

She kept her smile neutral. It wasn't the first time a man had undressed her with his eyes. Not Mo—at least not so blatantly—though he'd once undressed her with his hands. And she'd repaid the favor.

She took a sip of wine and greeted the other people at the table. Her favorite was Jackie, Leo's wife, an attractive blond with a blunt voice. Rosa liked her right from the first word.

Her least favorite was Theresa, Mo's ex, whose nostrils pinched as she nodded her chin at her, as if she were a princess and Rosa the pea under the first of her twenty mattresses.

Princess in her own mind, Rosa thought, smiling as she imagined Theresa's face turning into an ice sculpture. Theresa started, her eyes widening, then Rosa ignored her, glancing around the table. Everything looked just as it should, but one person was missing.

Music came on over the speakers, Andrea Bocelli singing a love song in Italian.

She wanted to put her head down and cry, and she didn't know why.

"Where's Bobby?" she asked.

Mo and Leo chuckled. Jackie honked with laughter.

Gina, a big-haired brunette, shot Jackie a look that should've made her drop dead to the floor.

"He wanted to stay for dinner with his jailors." Gina bit out the words.

Everyone except Gina was grinning or trying to hide a smile. Rosa decided that she would hear about what happened later, and she speared a grilled eggplant and a *Gamberi Pancetta*, which was char grilled-pancetta-wrapped shrimp. There were two more Italian appetizers, but as much as she wanted to eat it all, she couldn't. Everything looked so good. Her son and his girlfriend were geniuses in the kitchen. She knew their dishes were going to be amazing. If she wasn't choosy, she'd end up sleeping in one of the booths that lined the wall, too weak to pull her overstuffed body up the steps to her apartment.

And who would take care of the kittens?

She sipped wine and listened to the music. Andrea Bocelli's voice stirred her heart, and the smell of the food stirred her appetite. Mo sat no closer to her than Earl, but Mo stirred another appetite, her skin prickling and heating.

She didn't know what was happening to her.

Actually she did know, but it certainly shouldn't happen here.

She did what any woman would do. Took two gulps of wine.

The second course came, the servings much smaller than was normal at most Italian restaurants in the US. She chose Calamari alla Manfredi, which was warm salad with calamari. Earl chose the Minestrone and Mo the Prosciutto e Funghi, which was ravioli in creamy sauce of prosciutto and mushrooms.

Conversation slowed as everyone dug in, and at one

point, all Rosa heard was hums of appreciation. She let Mo taste a forkful of her calamari, and she took a bite of his ravioli. Eating off his plate seemed like a natural thing to do.

Something was building inside her. Not about the food. An emotion. Something she didn't want to look at or examine too closely. Not now. She was eating and talking. She was looking at everyone's expressions so that she could describe to Matt and Zoe the bliss on their faces as they ate.

But the emotion wouldn't go away. It was there inside her, hovering around her. A thickness in the air. And her skin warmed and at the same time shivered, and she felt warm and shivery inside, too.

She finished the calamari, and Lisa asked if she wanted soup or the other dish. She shook her head then gulped the last of the wine. In less than five seconds, Lisa was back with a wine bottle, refilling her glass. It was too late to stop her, but Rosa didn't have to drink it. She grabbed the ice water instead and gulped down a quarter of it, her head back.

After setting it on the table, she glanced up and saw everyone looking at her.

Her gaze shifted to Mo. He stared into her eyes then smiled. His brown eyes seemed heated, like melted chocolate.

"Oh no," she said.

"Oh no, what?" he asked, and his voice rasped across her nerve ends.

She shook her head and looked forward at Leo, but he was saying something to Jackie that made her laugh too loudly, and he grinned at her, the spark in his eyes making Rosa think, despite his other women, these two humped like bunnies—only longer and much better.

In her periphery, Mo leaned toward her. The next instant, his hand clutched her thigh.

She gasped before she could stop herself. People looked at her, and she smiled and peered around, as if trying to see what they were looking at. As soon as they started talking, eating, and drinking, she reached beneath the tablecloth and tried to lift Mo's hand. He resisted.

Leaning toward him, she murmured, "Would you like me to stick a fork in the back of your hand?"

He chuckled...and still his hand was on her thigh, kneading it. Moving up to the juncture at the top of her thigh.

Oh God, oh God, oh God...

Brenda and Lisa took away the dishes. Mo removed his hand.

She immediately missed it. Scolding herself didn't change the pleasure his touch had given her.

The next course started. Like the others, these were served on smaller plates than normal. Rosa had the Fettucine Capasnte e Funghi, which was pan-seared jumbo sea scallops over pasta with sautéed wild mushrooms with truffle oil. It was Matt's dish, and she loved everything about it. Across the table, Jackie enthused about the chicken parmesan.

"Mo," she called loudly, as if Mo was sitting across the room instead of across the table. "I've had chicken parmesan thousands of times—I've made it hundreds of times—and this is the best I've had. You'll have to thank the chef for me."

"I think it's wonderful, too, but you can thank the chef yourself." He gestured to Rosa.

Jackie loudly told her how much she enjoyed it. Rosa said she'd be happy to email Jackie her recipe. Jackie blessed her, and the others in the Jersey crowd except for Theresa took a plate of the chicken parmesan.

Rosa went back to eating her scallop dish, but the emotion from before was back inside her, choking her, making it hard to swallow when she felt so much. Making it hard to sit next to Mo, because her body was responding to his, even though he wasn't touching her anymore. He didn't have to touch her. It was enough that he was just here in this room. It was enough that he sat next to her, his heat reaching out to her then back at him then back to her. An exquisite loop of desire.

Oh God, oh God, oh God...

She jumped up, her chair pushed back on the old wooden floor. Aware of everyone staring at her again, she forced her lips to turn up. "Excuse me," she said then hurried away, letting them think she was leaving for the usual reasons.

They would have no clue that she left because she was finally beginning to understand the emotion. It was like a liquid heating in a pan, too thin to be soup. But if she kept the pot on the burner it would thicken until she could see the magic moment that said, yes, it was soup.

This emotion, she thought as she hurried down the short hall that led to the men's and women's rooms, was reaching the magic moment, and she didn't want to believe what the emotion was, but she couldn't deny it. Not anymore. Not with the way it surged higher and higher inside her until she was inhaling and exhaling it.

Her heart beat in rhythm to it.

Her blood pulsed to it.

Love.

For.

Mo.

She loved him. But she didn't want to. This...thing

they had...she'd always said it was temporary.

And what about him? It was certainly temporary to him. He had his son now and wouldn't want her around. He didn't even want the cats, both of them staying with her, though Checkers was unofficially his.

But none of these arguments changed her emotions as she headed into the ladies' bathroom, because emotions were too stupid to listen to lectures on why they shouldn't feel something. They just cared how they felt. They just said, *Have another glass of wine, then brush your hand on his leg and see what happens.*

Right. Like sex helped anything. Sometimes sex was as dangerous as texting while driving. The best thing for her to do was keep her knees closed when he was nearby and try to think of something else. Chocolate. Spaghetti. One of Katie's delicious pies.

With a strangled laugh, she washed her hands and looked at herself in the mirror. In her dress, she looked put together and almost elegant.

But perhaps there was something in her eyes... A wild darkness. She laughed, hearing the high pitch—

The door opened. She looked sideways, and her breath shuddered. "This isn't the men's room."

Mo stepped inside, letting the door swing shut behind him. "I know what room it is. What happened in there? Something upset you."

"*You* happened." She faced him. Best to say it and get it done. She'd never been a coward and wasn't going to start now.

"Me?" He stepped backward, his butt hitting the door. "I'm the one making you unhappy?" His head shook, and she could feel his sadness. "That's the last thing I want to do."

Looking at his face, seeing the intensity leave him, she

felt like she was in an alternate universe.

He turned. "Don't worry, I'll leave you alone from now on."

"Wait a minute!" She grabbed his arm. He stopped mid-turn and looked at her. Her breath stuck in her throat at what she thought she saw. She wanted it to be true so badly that she was afraid to ask.

But she'd always conquered her fear by forging ahead and doing what scared her. "You love me," she said in a husky whisper.

Though she didn't make it a question, he nodded. "I desired you from the first moment I saw you. It had turned to love long before you started working for me."

A small cry came out of her throat then her knees went weak.

He loved her. He *loved* her. Joy rose inside her like she imagined the sea rose up beneath Noah's ark. She wanted to float up to the ceiling. She wanted to dance, to sing, to laugh. But all she could do was smile like a clown on happy pills.

"I love you, too," she said.

And then she couldn't say anything more because they were kissing. He was holding her close, and all that emotion had her holding him just as tightly. They had too many clothes on, but she had just enough sense not to start whipping them off. And so did he, because he let go of her and stood back.

And his eyes...

Were those tears?

"Why did you scare me?" he asked. "Why did you pull away?"

"Because I was afraid of being hurt." She crossed her hands over her breastbone and could feel the pounding of her heart. "Mike's betrayal did something to my confidence. And these feelings for you came too soon. I wasn't ready."

"We can take it slow."

"Only if you want to."

"I've been in love with you for months. That's not changing."

She shook her head. "Let's talk about this later. We have guests, and you'd better go back. I'll be there in a minute."

He frowned, and she made shooing gestures and laughed, hearing the shaky note in her voice. "I'm not putting you off or changing my mind. I'll be there in a minute. I'm just not ready to tell everyone."

He nodded and left. She looked at herself in the mirror again. She hadn't worn lipstick, but her lips looked rosy from their kissing. "You love him," she whispered. Then she put her hands up in the air and did a little dance. Only then did she leave and had to stop herself from skipping like a child.

As she rounded the tables a moment later, heading toward Mo, someone knocked on the front door by the bar. Immediately two chairs scraped back, and the two bodyguards who'd sat at the end of the table jumped to their feet, one of the chairs knocked to the floor. Rosa's breath sucked in as she stared at the guns in their hands.

"No!" Gina staggered to her feet. "Put your guns away, you idiots! That has to be Bobby."

Then she ran toward the front entrance, the two men racing after her.

Mo was on his feet, and so were Sam and Leo. The others stood more slowly. Gina reached the entranceway first, her breath coming out in small sobs. Ignoring the men yelling at her to back up, she turned the lock, the sharp click audible even above the music, and wrenched the door open.

Rosa stared at the backs of Gina and the bodyguards frozen in place. As if they were staring at an alien or an angel. Something they had never expected to see. All Rosa could see was the backs of the two broad bodyguards and a slice of Gina's backside.

Rosa put her leg out to step forward. Mo's arm snaked out to hold her back as Gina shouted, "Who the hell are you?"

"Katie Guthrie. A friend of Mo's. Is he here?"

Sam, Katie's dad, strode toward the bar area, Mo after him.

"She's my daughter," Sam snapped, his normal gravelly voice commanding. "Put your weapons away right now."

Both men glanced behind Sam at Leo. Whatever they saw made them lower the guns and step back.

Gina made a disgusted noise and stomped back to the table. Rosa looked at the backs of the two men already at the door. She could see just enough of Katie to glimpse a pie box in her hands. Probably the reason the two bodyguards remained, their guns pointing at the floor but not put away. Afraid she was carrying a bomb in the pie box.

"I had to bring the pie," Katie said.

"Okay, then you're coming in." Sam turned to Mo. "That okay?"

"Katie, you're always welcome in my place." Mo gave the bodyguards a dark look. "Back off. She's okay."

Sam took his daughter's arm and led her toward the table. Rosa stood behind her chair while Sam, Katie, and Mo stopped at the end of the table.

"Katie's our pie maker," Elsa said, her voice clear. "She's also a YouTube video star. She contributed a pie for dinner. You'll have to try it."

"Pie maker and video star?" Amusement glittered in Leo's eyes. He raised his voice. "We're just about to have dessert. Sit down and join us. Mo, grab a chair for the little pie maker."

Rosa grimaced. Katie's expression was serious tonight.

"You brought another pie?" Jackie called out. "Didn't you think Mo had enough desserts?"

"I'm sorry for crashing the dinner party." Katie's cheeks flushed with color. "I just had this need to bake a pie. I thought it was for tomorrow, but..." She glanced at Rosa then Mo.

"You brought a pie for one of us?" he asked.

She nodded. "This pie is for two people. That's never happened before."

"Who?" Mo stepped back until he was at Rosa's side, as if he was thinking the same thing as her. The same prickles of expectation.

Katie stepped toward them, holding the pie box. "For you and Rosa."

"What is it?" Rosa asked as Mo took the pie.

"Oh, it's a new one with coconut and banana and—"

"No." Rosa pushed up from her chair. "What's it called?"

Katie's forehead creased, and she looked at the table.

"You can say it here," Mo said, and Rosa heard the grin in his voice. Katie shot her a questioning look, and she felt her face warm.

Then Mo looked at her, and in his face, she saw a question, too. Saw that he wondered if she really meant what she'd said in the bathroom. If she would change her mind.

Moisture welled up in her eyes for him. After all he'd been through, someone should cry for him. His friends turning on him. His wife lying. And then what had she done? Her uncertainties had made her step back from him, too.

He deserved better...and so did she.

She smiled at him then nodded Katie to go ahead.

"I call it the Love Pie," Katie said.

Laughter broke out, and someone gasped—Mo's ex-wife, Rosa thought. Mo didn't look at Theresa. He handed the pie back to Katie, took Rosa in his arms and kissed her. Not a long kiss but long enough for her to clasp her arms around him and kiss him back.

Then they were apart and smiling at each other, not wanting to take their gazes away from their lover's face.

"Does this mean you're not coming back to Jersey?" Leo asked.

"No way," Mo said, grinning so wide Rosa thought his cheeks must hurt.

Around the table, people talked at once, laughter in the air. From the speakers, Andrea Bocelli started another love song.

"You're sure?" Mo asked, his voice low.

She put her hand on his cheek. "My heart is yours."

He didn't kiss her again, but love shone from his eyes. She felt weepy again, but a good weepiness, coming from an overload of happiness.

The rest of the evening passed quickly. Katie stayed for dessert, and Leo and Jackie pronounced her ricotta pie the best they'd ever eaten. She told them she'd planned to make something else, but then she'd been compelled to make that instead. She said it was a "Happy Memories Pie."

Leo's face went still. "It made me think of my nonna."

Jackie put her arm around him. "Me too," she said, her voice soft for once.

It was still light out when one of the bodyguards bent over Leo's shoulder and murmured something. Leo announced they needed to part but would like to see the chefs first.

When Matt and Zoe came out, he praised their cooking, then asked when they'd be through with their culinary college. When they said this was their last year, he said he'd come into possession of a restaurant and would be looking for some good chefs. One of the bodyguards gave them each a card and said to call him.

They left with doggy bags, planning to pick up Bobby on the way.

The locals left, too, saying it was the most interesting night they'd ever had.

Mo told Brenda and Lisa he was giving them a bonus, and they said Jackie had given them each two hundred dollars and told them if they ever wanted to come to Jersey, she could use them in their new restaurant.

They left, talking to each other, their voices high and excited. Mo went into the dishwashing room to say something to Tim the busboy. Dario and Rosa broke up the long table into four small tables.

"It was a good night," Dario said, his voice a little awkward.

Taking it as approval, Rosa touched his shoulder and agreed that it was a very good night. "No one got killed," she added.

Dario was still chuckling as they reached the kitchen where Tim was shoving something in his wallet and so was Matt, while Zoe was smiling up at Mo as if she were looking at Santa Claus. Sniffing, she said this was the best night of her life.

While Tim finished the dishes, the five of them sat in the front and drank a bottle of wine and talked about food and the village. Then Tony came by. He turned down a glass of wine, saying he was driving Matt and Zoe to the airport.

Rosa hugged all three of them before they left.

Then it was just the three of them inside. Dario looked at her and Mo, and his expression was grave. As if he wondered where he fit in this new life.

More love welled up in Rosa, so big and so bright and so intense, she felt the love streaming out of her pores straight to him. She held out her arms.

"You'll be my fourth son," she said.

And then they were hugging, she and Dario. Over his shoulder she saw Mo looking at her with something in his eyes that said he wasn't done yet.

43

Mo loved his son. He would die for his son. Ever since Dario had come to Miracle, he thanked God about one hundred times a day.

But right now, he wished to hell Dario would get up from the recliner in his living room and go to bed.

Something happened downstairs just before they came up. He'd seen the change in Rosa's face. One second she'd been glowing. The next her light had dimmed.

She got up from the couch next to him. "I should go to bed. It was a great day, guys."

"You're staying here tonight," Mo said.

"The kittens—"

"They have water, food, and a litter box. They'll be fine where they are. Tomorrow we can move them here."

She gave him The Stare.

He arched his left eyebrow at her. Her stare made him want to kiss her. But pretty much everything she did made him want to kiss her. "There's plenty of room here for you."

Her gaze flicked to Dario and back. "I have plenty of room in my apartment already," she said, but her normal fire was missing.

"This isn't because of me, is it?" Dario said. "I'm not a kid. I've seen the way you two look at each other." He gestured with his hands up. "I'm glad you're making my dad happy."

"You're sure?" She stared at him, as if her happiness hinged on what he was going to say next.

"I don't lie." His smooth forehead furrowed. "Not about important things."

"I have a very smart son." Mo grinned at Dario, the son he'd loved and nurtured and had thought he'd lost.

Dario grinned back then hopped off the recliner. "I'm off to bed. I ate so much that any noises coming from the bedroom won't wake me."

Mo laughed and Rosa shrank down on the sofa and moaned. Dario strode down the hall to the bedroom, chuckling.

"Is that it?" Mo turned to Rosa. "You were worried about Dario?"

"I know, it's silly. I've just..." She flapped her hands in the air and gazed at him, this strong woman he'd fallen in love with, and he loved her just as much even when her forehead was creased with uncertainty. "It feels like I won the life lottery. I have you and my wonderful children. Even Nick... He's with his dad and isn't perfect, but people told me he was on Main Street the other day, ready to protect you."

Mo sat next to her and nodded, though he thought perhaps Nick didn't want to look like an asshole in front of his friends. But he was smart enough not to say that to the woman he loved.

"And now, I have..." Tears glittering in her eyes, she put her hand on Mo's left chest. "This. I have this."

He put his hand over hers, holding it over his heart. "You will always have this."

"It's so much like my best dream, and I guess I'm afraid if I embrace it, it will go away."

"If you try to embrace it..." He released her and twisted to put his arms around her. "I promise you, nothing will go away. Instead it just might get harder."

She chuckled, the glitter in her eyes changing to a

glow. "I thought you were tired."

"Not anymore. You revived me."

"Oh my." She smiled at him. "Already I'm seeing the benefits of living with a younger man."

"Married to."

She jerked out of his embrace. "What?"

"I want to marry you."

"I am married."

"Not for long."

She nodded but stayed silent.

A cold shiver spiked through him and he sat straight. "Do you want to marry me?"

"Yes." She smiled. Then she smiled wider. Then she laughed and nodded her head. "Yes! Yes, yes, yes!"

"We'll have another feast," he said. "For the whole village."

"Remember we promised them a feast?" She still smiled. Glowing at him. "Late spring or summer at Miracle Lake. Let's do it then."

He got up and held out his hand. She took it and he pulled her up. "Let's go to bed."

"Where you will get even harder," she said, laughing.

In the hall, he let her go ahead of him. She was still smiling and so was he. Like her, he felt as if he'd won the life lottery. When he'd left Jersey, he'd thought he'd never be happy again. Now he was happier than he'd ever been.

Maybe it had taken a miracle.

Or maybe it was just love.

He followed her into the bedroom and closed the door behind him.

Hearts in Motion

A Rescued Heart novel

Unedited excerpt

Abby had known she'd have to see Holden Ramsay again. That he was coming to pick up Cara and, in the future, would be dropping her off in the mornings. If not for the girl's sad little face, Abby might have smiled at his aunt and made her apologies.

That and the fact that she desperately needed the money. His aunt's proposal was an answer to her prayers. Enough to pay a few bills and get them over this hard time.

Only two weeks...

By then she would think of something to keep them going. Something to save them all.

She crossed her arms and leaned against the door jamb.

He hadn't changed. A face like that could be on a movie poster. A chin that looked stubborn. A line permanently creased into his forehead. Brows slashed above silvery blue eyes that made her feel as if he were peering into her soul.

"Well, if it isn't the Big Bad Wolf at my door," she said.

His face that had been set in hard lines made a lightning change to surprise. So he finally remembered her. The lower half of his face opened into a grin, and she thought it was like watching a large rock crack in half.

Still looking at him, she amended that to a very handsome rock.

"Do you really want me to say the Big Bad Wolf's reply, Little Red?"

She groaned, though she'd asked for it. When would she learn to keep her mouth shut? So what if keeping her mouth shut was boring? She could be boring.

But not today.

She pushed away from the door jamb. "Only if you want to get your shin kicked."

"Hard to resist that line. I could take my chances."

"And I could kick higher."

He laughed again and shook his head. "You have an odd effect on me."

"Join the crowd." She gestured behind him, as if hundreds of confused, invisible people milled there, afraid to get too close to her. "So you are human. That's not what I've been hearing."

"I'm sure it's nothing Derrick ever said about me."

"It was a long time ago that I dated your brother for a glorious ten days." She rolled her eyes, though there was a small ache in her chest. Not for Derrick. For her parents, who'd laughed when she fumed at them about Derrick and his brother, until she'd laughed, too. One of her last memories of them.

She tamped the ache down. She preferred to think they were still alive somewhere, in another dimension, perhaps. Maybe just a breath away, sending her and Grace love. Telling her not to let the city's multi-millionaire overwhelm her.

As if.

"My brother's an asshole," he said.

"No arguments." She grinned. "You said the same thing when I went to your house and asked for my physics book back."

"Demanded it back. Said you were going to call the police on Derrick if I didn't get it for you." He lowered his head to peer down at her, reminding her that her feet were bare, and she was at least ten inches shorter than his six foot or more height.

She straightened her spine. "And you told me to go ahead and call the police."

He chuckled.

"You got the book for me anyway."

"I was afraid you would combust in my mother's foyer if I didn't. How did you do in your physics class, anyway?"

She opened the screen door. "Like I said, a long time ago. Come on in."

HEARTS IN MOTION, the first novel of Edie's Rescued Hearts series, will be released in July.

About Edie Ramer

Edie Ramer is funnier on the page than in real life. A multiple award-winning writer, she writes stories with heart, attitude, and magic. She lives in southeastern Wisconsin with her husband, dog and one important cat.

Connect with Edie Online

www.edieramer.com
https://twitter.com/edieramer
http://www.facebook.com/edieramer.author

www.ingramcontent.com/pod-product-compliance
Lightning Source LLC
Chambersburg PA
CBHW071140170626
46809CB00002B/696